The Holly House Mystery

By the same author

The Seafront Corpse
A Seaside Mourning
A Christmas Malice
Speak for the Dead

Copyright © A. and J. Bainbridge 2015/2021
The right of Anne Bainbridge to be identified as the author of this work has been asserted by her in accordance with the Copyright, Designs and Patent Act 1988. All rights reserved. No part of this publication may be reproduced, stored in or introduced into a retrieval system, or transmitted, in any form, or by any means (electronic, mechanical, photocopying, recording or otherwise) without the prior written permission of the author. Any person who does any unauthorised act in relation to this publication may be liable to criminal prosecution and civil claims for damages. Brief quotations for review purposes are an exemption to the above. This publication must not be circulated in any form of binding or cover other than that in which it is now published and without a similar condition including this condition being imposed on the subsequent purchaser. © Cover Picture: Fotolia.

All characters in this novel are fictitious and any resemblance to real persons, living or dead, is purely coincidental.

THE HOLLY HOUSE MYSTERY

An Inspector Chance Mystery

Anne Bainbridge

Gaslight Crime

One

December 1931

Across the moonlit gardens, beyond the shadow of a ruined arch, the body lay undiscovered all night. A crimson brown stain dried like a question mark on the cold forehead.

The big house, on the edge of the village, was as enclosed over Christmas as in the centuries when it had been the site of a medieval priory. Snow had been lying on the South Downs for several days. The bare, rounded hills reaching like a spine across a stretch of Sussex, were as smooth and gleaming as royal icing. The silvery river looping around the grounds made an island of the old place. A wooden footbridge to the meadows was impassable and the stone bridge through the ancient gatehouse, barred until morning.

Earlier that night

A lamp still burned in the hall, throwing the shadow of the Christmas tree branches against the panelling as Tate made his last rounds before bed. The long room never quite felt empty to his mind. Not with the suit of armour standing like a silent presence in the recess by the oak staircase.

Mr. Mayhew couldn't resist raising the empty visor when the guests went up to change for dinner. The sprig of holly Miss Freda had fixed in one of the gauntlets was like spots of blood against the gleaming metal.

He'd already seen that they were locked up. It remained only to check that nothing had been overlooked in the downstairs rooms. The fire-guards were in place, cigarette-boxes refilled and playing cards put away. In the drawing-room, Mrs Terry had once again left her spectacle-case down the side of her habitual arm-chair.

Mr. Vernon had been showing the Athertons his collection of curios in the library. Tate secured the glass lid. The weapons were worth something, a handsome flintlock, a couple of daggers and a tiny ladies' muff pistol. But clay pipes and musket balls, an old catapult, bits of tile and pottery, neatly-labelled rubbish if you asked him. Mr. Atherton, who'd seen them before, was enthusiastic as always. His new missus yawned delicately like a cat.

Outside, the moon was nearly full, casting an eerie light over the rose garden. The ruins were outlined against the night sky and the snowy lawns glistened. Tate let the curtain fall and retired to their rooms at the back of the house.

Hilda was sitting on the edge of the bed with a hair-pin between her lips. Forcing her hair into flat curls, as she did every night without needing the mirror. When she'd pinned all over her scalp, she fitted on her hair-net, like a tight cover on a pot of her jam.

'All gone up at last, have they?'

'I had to wait for them to finish their billiards.'

'All right for those who don't have to be up early.' Hilda Tate yawned as she settled beneath the eiderdown. 'That's Boxing Day over for another year, I'm tired out. I thought it all went off very well.'

'You did them proud, same as always.'

'The vicar enjoyed his dinner. Popped in the kitchen to thank me personally.'

'I shouldn't say it, I know,' Tate hung up his tie and emptied his pockets. 'But I reckon we'll do handsomely when they leave. Mr. Atherton's always very appreciative. And Mr. Vernon knows how much extra work there is when we've house-guests. Haven't had a Christmas box yet. He'll be waiting till this week's over.'

'We shouldn't count our chickens, Bill. Still, you're probably right. I've filled you a bottle, so don't stub your toes.'

'Ta, love.' The springs creaked as he bent to unlace his shoes. 'It's freezing out there. Shouldn't think even the dead monk'd fancy haunting on a night like this.'

Next morning

Elsie Ruddock was living for the moment when she could peel off her stockings and dab some ointment on her chilblains. No good cycling in this weather. She'd worn thick knitted socks inside her galoshes and her feet had still been like blocks of ice. Now levered in her black courts, her toes were stinging like a bed of nettles.

The breakfast-room should have been cleared away long since but the last of the guests wasn't down. She'd been trotting back and forth with fresh tea and coffee, replenishing the hot dishes and there was a mountain of crocks to be washed up.

She didn't mind obliging when Mr. Vernon had house-guests. The extra was welcome but the gentry had some consideration. They didn't make even more work when they could help it.

She was waiting for Mrs Atherton. Three mornings running, she'd been last down and this was her latest yet. Yesterday, she'd wondered in, lifted all the lids and left them off, then asked for scrambled eggs. The one thing you couldn't leave lying around in a chafing dish, not unless you wanted it to taste like rubber.

Crepe-de-chine underwear and diamonds you'd kill for, didn't mean top drawer. Too much show by half. It wasn't done to dress up in the country.

Mrs Terry knew that without thinking. A nice twinset for indoors and her single row of pearls for the evening, even if it was all she had. She wouldn't have dreamt of draping herself like a Christmas tree. Same with Miss Freda, her best green foulard and those long amber beads, very suitable. Granted, she wasn't a beauty but they set off her colouring. Someone should tell that Mrs Atherton, blondes shouldn't wear green. Not even when they got it out of a bottle.

'It's all go this morning.' Bridget nudged open the scullery door with a loaded tray. 'The gentlemen are feeling a bit cooped up. They're talking about going for a walk in the snow. Miss Freda's on about setting up the archery target. What with the Boxing Day Meet being cancelled, the guests have had nothing to look at in the village.'

'Their whole life's one round of entertainment, if you ask me.'

'That's not fair. Miss Freda has a job and Mrs Terry has her charity work.

'I don't mean our ladies.' She rolled up her sleeves.

'Oh, you mean Mrs Atherton. You should see her lovely things but she doesn't hang them up. She was probably used to a dresser, they call it, don't they? P'raps she thought she'd get a ladies-maid here.'

'Them days are gone, apart from the titled. Even Mr. Tate's not a butler like they were before the War.' Elsie ran the water with unnecessary force. 'Dresser, my foot, they're only for leading ladies. I've never heard of her. Mr. Atherton's a nice gentleman, always speaks very respectful. A man like that doesn't stand a chance, once her type's got her claws in.'

'You can't say he isn't happy. He can't do enough for her. Mrs Atherton was telling the mistress, he's promised her a motor-car of her own, a runabout, she said. I'd best get back. You haven't seen Nora in your travels, have you?'

'Not yet, isn't she upstairs?'

Bridget shook her head. 'She must be down here. I haven't seen sight nor sound of her since she said good-night. Unless she's slept in? She's picked her time when we've extra rooms to do. I'd better go and check.'

'What's that needs checking?' Mrs Tate came through from the kitchen, wiping her hands.

'It's Nora, neither of us have seen her this morning.'

'Come to think of it, I haven't either. I thought she'd started on the beds. Pop up to her room, Bridget. See if she's poorly.'

'She's outside.'

They turned to see a figure in the doorway, wearing snow-crusted brogues.

'Oh, Miss Freda, the…' Mrs Tate, prepared to be reproachful about her floor, let her voice trail away. 'Whatever is it? You look white as a sheet.'

'It's Nora. We've just found her... outside. There's been a terrible accident. I'm afraid she's dead.'

'Dead? How can she be?' Elsie stepped forward. She glanced at Bridget, with her mouth fit to catch flies.

'Are you sure? Where is she?' Mrs Tate took the young woman by the arm.

'Over by the ruins. You know where the smashed column is? She's hit her head on one of the stones. Yes, she's quite dead.'

'Not those horrible great lumps? But that's the same as the old ghost story. I've come over all queer.' She slumped against the cupboard.

'Hush, Elsie.'

'I've always said they should have been took away before someone broke their neck on them. What was she doing outside, this time of the morning?'

'For goodness sake, will you hold your tongue? Come and sit down, Miss. Bridget, fetch the brandy. It's what I use for cooking but it's quicker. You're in shock, a nip'll do you the world of good.'

'You're very kind, Mrs T. but I mustn't. Mr. Mayhew was with me. He's gone to get Dr. Hurst, not that he can do anything and P.C. Pickard. I must get back to Nora. And someone must tell my uncle.'

'I can do that for you, Miss, you're shaking. Put your head between your knees if you feel sick.'

Freda Terry pushed her dark hair away from her brow. 'Someone should be with her. I need a blanket. It doesn't seem decent to leave her uncovered like that. She's lying on the snow with her hands upwards as though she's asking for help. In blue woolly gloves. It's all rather ghastly. I made Basil close her eyes. They were staring up at us.'

~

The rumpled newspaper landed on the carpet. Plunging share-prices, pay-cuts and dole queues, none of which were a worry in his line but sobering stuff, all the same. The season of goodwill was apparent only in advertisements for Christmas shows and January sales.

'You're getting chubby,' Inspector Eddie Chance said. 'I'm surprised you haven't been sick, tucking into that pastry.'

In police terms, he was an accessory. He wasn't a fussy eater but drew the line at his mother-in-law's leaden mince pies. They had to be disposed of somehow. His accomplice appeared to have a cast-iron stomach and wasn't going to spill the beans. He blinked at Chance and stretched.

'Let's make the most of it, chum. While we've got the place to ourselves.'

Rousing himself from his arm-chair, he carefully removed a record from its sleeve and adjusted the gramophone needle.

'Cheers,' he said to Douglas, sipping his glass of Scotch. Blended - Stella didn't see the point in paying extra -but a welcome Christmas present, all the same. The strains of a lively cornet breezed around the living-room.

'I bet you can afford a single malt.' Chance said. He raised an eyebrow at the open magazine, also lying on the carpet. Douglas Fairbanks, the cat's namesake smirked back, leaning elegantly by a Hollywood mantelpiece. A new check slipper covered his face.

He refused to admit to more than tolerating Douglas, the tabby they'd taken in last summer. As he'd pointed out at the time, someone always needed homes for a litter and they'd managed perfectly well all these years without a mouser. Stella had pointed out that they now lived in a quiet road and had a proper garden. Daphne and Vic had waded in. He'd pointed out that a cat would ruin their nylons, in the case of his wife and daughter.

A pesky kitten had duly turned up in a basket and rubbed his way into everyone's affections but his. In the contrary way of cats, he'd taken to sitting by him when he was trying to read the newspaper, the only human who didn't fawn over him. At least Douglas didn't mind jazz, if his approving purr was anything to go by.

Chance sprawled back, idly contemplating the Christmas tree. A scattering of pine needles decorated the carpet. He knew he'd be expected to plant the wretched fir in the garden. The lowest branches were bare, since Douglas had taken to patting the baubles, and the fairy had had a hard life.

Greetings cards were strung along the wall and paper-chains looped across the ceiling. Even the snow was jolly when viewed from beside the fire. It was freezing upstairs. Daphne had reverted several years and helped Vic build a snow-man in the front garden. The others had gone to the pantomime, leaving him in blissful peace.

Shutting his eyes, Chance drifted with the music. It was some twenty minutes later when he realised that the discordant notes intruding on the saxophone were coming from the beastly telephone-bell in the hall.

~

Sidney Godwin whistled while he stowed his bag of tricks in the boot. His hastily packed grip was already in. The snow had been scraped clear as far as the street, shovelled either side of grubby tyre tracks. As he hadn't been driving long, he intended to take it cautiously up the hill, where he was to pick up the inspector.

The door to the yard opened and the desk-sergeant poked his head out.

'I don't know what you're sounding so cheerful about. It's enough to freeze the whatsits off a brass monkey.'

'It's not much better inside, Sarge.'

'Don't I know it. It's proper parky behind that desk.'

Godwin grinned to himself. There was a toasting fork propped by the gas-fire out the back and Inspector Forrest's wife had sent in a Christmas cake for them all. He'd noticed a plate with marzipan crumbs discreetly behind the cards.

Tennysham police-station was looking quite festive. Someone had even stuck a sprig of mistletoe over the door to the C.I.D. room. Their sole W.P.C. had promptly climbed on a stool and snatched it down. Only the drawing-pin remained.

'To think this time yesterday, I was stuck with the wife's relatives.' The sergeant rubbed his hands. 'I was expecting it to be a lot quieter here till New Year's Eve, put my name down specially. Not even a drunk sleeping it off, then we go and get the Chief Constable on the blower. Gawd knows what it'll be like on the Downs. You sorry you've been landed with this, Sid?'

He was rather looking forward to it, Godwin thought, a few minutes later. Which was rotten actually, a young girl had been done in. He had the High Street to himself as he crawled along, the entrance to the Arcade barred and the mannequins in Grove's window display, blank-faced in their furs. Only Woolworths looked merry with cheap and cheerful Chinese lanterns, toys and gaudy tinsel.

Outside the Alex, bright posters announced the Players' Christmas panto. The matinee of Jack and the Beanstalk was well under way. Tickets until January had been sold out for ages. His family would be going at the week-end. Possibly, he wouldn't be joining them now. It was worse somehow, to have a murder this time of year. He shook his head. The youngest member of the team, he might be, but too old to believe only good things happened at Christmas.

The rear of Tennysham rose, from the flat town centre and promenade, to the new streets going up on the hill. As Godwin turned the steering-wheel into Hever Drive, he saw Inspector Chance waiting on the pavement. A burly figure in tweed overcoat and trilby, hands shoved in his pockets, he was pacing up and down. Never a one to wait patiently, that didn't bode well.

He was pleasantly surprised when Chance climbed in next to him and remarked cheerfully, 'No peace for the wicked, Godwin.'

'Afternoon, sir. I say, that's a jolly snow-man.'

'My son's handiwork. I hadn't finished with that hat.'

'Have you been having a good Christmas, sir?'

The inspector grunted, which was more usual. 'Not for men, is it? I was enjoying the first spot of peace and quiet I'd had in days, mind. Ah, well, duty calls. Know the way?'

'I do to Ockendon, sir. Holly House sounds appropriate, doesn't it?'

'Eh?'

'Holly, sir, Christmassy, like robins and snow and mistletoe.'

'Oh, you were the wag who stuck that up, were you? Not altogether fair on young Phyllis.'

He felt his cheeks warming, despite the cold, the curse of ginger hair. 'Not me, sir, I wouldn't do that. Are we going straight to the scene?'

'No, the police-house first, we're liaising with the local man. What's the hold-up?'

Keeping calm, he tried again. 'Sorry, the gear's a bit stiff.' Out of the corner of his eye, he saw the inspector regard him dubiously. 'Is the local chap putting us up, sir?'

'Not likely. Didn't Sergeant Lelliott say? The bobby's booking us in the village pub. The Chief Constable seemed to think we might be unable to go back and forth if it snows any more. So, I hope you've packed a clean collar.'

With a fervent prayer that they had two rooms, Godwin set off. The driving-gloves his mother had given him were clenched on the steering-wheel.

Chance rubbed at the window and sighed. 'Don't tell me you can't turn round?'

'Oh, I can, sir, not to worry. It's just easier to come out further up in this weather.'

'You don't inspire confidence on the Downs, Godwin. My unaccustomed seasonal good-will might have vanished by the time we get there.'

'We'll be fine, sir. I'm a careful driver. Fred Richards taught me.'

'Constable Richards drives like he's at Brooklands.'

Now his newly-acquired skill was vanishing like melting snow. The inspector didn't miss much. And he wasn't the sort of chap you could ask to get out and give you a push. He should have brought sacks in case the wheels got stuck.

'You haven't had a prang yet,' Chance conceded generously. 'But you're unaccustomed to snow.'

Winter had come in suddenly, the week before Christmas. On most years in Tennysham they could see the smudged white ridge of the Downs behind the resort, though rarely for long. The town streets might be covered for a few days but snow rarely reached the promenade with its salty air.

Tennysham was known on its railway posters for a mild climate, nearing the top in sunshine records and being a wintering-hole of elderly visitors. This year, snow had dusted the sea-front railings and icicles had been seen on outdoor lavs.

'How much did Sergeant Lelliott tell you?'

'That a young woman's been found dead in the grounds, one of the maids and foul play's suspected.'

'The owner of Holly House is a Mr. Clifford Vernon and to complicate matters, he's acquainted with friends of the Chief Constable.'

'Does that mean he's above suspicion, sir?'

'Not in my book, it doesn't. Though it would probably suit our betters if the butler did it.'

'How was the dead woman killed, sir?'

'Bashed on the temple, sometime last night. She wasn't found until late this morning. Apparently, it was taken for an accident at first. They thought she'd hit her head on some fallen masonry but the village doctor wasn't happy about the bruise.'

'He must be sharp. It sounds as though some doctors would have nodded it through.'

'Wouldn't be surprised. The murderer is probably cursing him.'

'Did no one hear the accident happen, sir?'

'The masonry didn't come from off the house. Wasn't the place originally a priory? There's an old gatehouse just past the village and that's the entrance. Anyway, that's all that's left, except for a few crumbling walls and some lumps of stone lying about the grounds. The body was found right by them. Sergeant Bishop could tell you about the place.'

'He'll be sorry to miss this, sir.'

Godwin wished the Sarge was with them, instead of enjoying his leave with his family in London. Known for his liking of old buildings, the inspector's number two was usually an affable go-between.

'Why anyone would want a collapsing ruin in their garden is beyond me ... Watch out!'

Braking with a jolt, he waited while a pheasant bobbed across the lane and into the skeletal hedgerow. Bright feathers stood out against the snow, its feet left wavering arrow marks. He wondered if there were footprints up to the body, or had fresh snow fallen to conceal them?

'It'll keep till we get there. *If* we get there. You keep your eyes on the road, Godwin. I don't want to end up in a ditch.'

'Will do, sir.' It was only about eighteen miles, he told himself.

It was going to be murder.

~

'Bloomin' typical.' P.C Pickard belched and rubbed his chest. 'Pardon. Can't enjoy Christmas week in peace. Even old Fly Carter'd be stopping in at nights till it thaws, I thought to myself, then this happens.'

'At least you can come in out of the cold now.'

'Not for long, they'll want me up at the big house with them. Him going rear over elbow wouldn't get me off to a good start. If I'd known, I wouldn't have indulged so much last night.'

'Here you are, then. You're not the only one who's had to run round unexpected, you know.'

He took the glass of liver salts his wife held out to him.

'Get that down you and stop mithering. That poor girl didn't die to put you out. Imagine if it was our Linda.'

'She'd have more sense than to go wandering about in the snow in middle of the night.'

'Did they agree to take him at the Pheasant?'

'It's all settled. They're wanting both rooms. He'll be bringing a constable with him.'

'We won't have to have them to supper, will we? Only I won't know what to say.'

'Not bloomin' likely, neither would I. No, they'll get their meals all-found. You'll have to see them though. They'll be making free with my office. Good job that's in order.'

'It'll be all right, Bert. I know you don't fancy dealing with an inspector from over at Tennysham but there's no avoiding it.'

'It's not that, though I'd sooner not take orders from someone the Chief Constable's brought in over our heads.'

'I've brushed your tunic and given your boots a quick rub over.' Meg Pickard went to pick up the jacket over the back of a chair. 'What's upsetting you? I can tell it's more than the C.I.D. coming.'

'I've been thinking, no one outside could have got into the grounds last night. If Dr. Hurst has it right, don't you see? It don't seem possible but...'

'What?' His wife held his jacket while he finished gulping.

'Stands to reason.' Thumping the glass on the kitchen table, he wiped his mouth. 'One of them up at Holly House must have done it.'

~

They met no one in the narrow lanes, seeing only a shepherd feeding his flock on lower pasture. Some red-faced children were sliding down a hill on tin trays, woolly scarves flying. A few, from better-off families, were dragging wooden sledges.

'What it is to be young,' Chance remarked. 'I don't like the look of that sky.'

The pale sunlight had been left by the sea. As they neared their destination, the sky was drained to a faint, yellowy sheen like oil in a puddle.

'Let's hope we're not stuck here for days.'

A black and white sign-post pointed the way to the village. Godwin hoped they wouldn't meet a motor coming up.

Ockendon was sheltered in the lee of the Downs, empty countryside stretching before them as they descended. Hedges, a river and distant railway line were lost in dips and bumps across the snowy landscape. Only copses stood out, their bare black branches casting dark shadows. On the outskirts of the village, a ragged line of crows watched from between telegraph poles.

'The entrance is on the other side,' Chance said. 'D'you ever come out this way?'

'Not really, sir. My father doesn't drive.'

'It's not my stamping ground either. We came through here last summer and stopped at a tea-garden. Make for the bobby's house. I could do with a cup while he fills us in on the suspects.'

'Right-oh. Does this Mr. Vernon have a job, sir?'

Opening his quarter-light, Chance flung his cigarette-end into the cold. 'Not as you or I would understand it. The Chief Constable says he writes histories. Shouldn't think there's a living in it so presumably, that translates as family money and that's his hobby.'

Godwin applied himself to looking out for the police-house, now they'd reached the main street. 'It doesn't seem to be on the green.'

'Well, it wouldn't be, would it? No room. This lot have been here for centuries. Try down there. It'll be tucked out of sight, along with the new council houses.'

'The pub looks pleasant, sir.'

'We'll see.'

They edged along a lane, spotting a small plain house with the familiar blue lamp.

As they got out, the front door opened and a middle-aged constable came to meet them. His stomach preceded the rest of him. The path was scraped bare and edged with a dirty snow-drift. A shovel leaned against the house wall and a woman stepped back from the window.

'Detective Inspector Chance, is it? Afternoon, sir.'

Godwin thought of a strange dog who doesn't know whether to wag his tail or scarper.

'Constable.' Chance gave him an appraising look. 'You are...?'

'Pickard, sir. Albert.'

'Been in the village long?'

'Must be twelve years, sir.'

'Good. You'll be able to tell us about the set-up at Holly House.'

Pickard tugged the knot of his tie. 'I'll do my best, sir but I don't know about all of them.'

'This is Detective Constable Godwin.'

'How do.'

He gave the bobby a friendly grin. They were bound to be an unwelcome intrusion. Pickard probably dreaded Chance being a stickler who'd go through all his paperwork while he was there. He was safer than he knew.

They were soon installed in the front room that served for officialdom, with a pot of tea and a wedge of Dundee cake apiece. An unpleasant reek of paraffin and singeing dust meant it wasn't cosy but at least, thought Godwin, he'd got them there.

'You'll be wanting to view the body before I take you up to see Mr. Vernon, sir?'

'It's been moved, I suppose? Where is it now?'

'Over at the doctor's surgery, that's just off the green. It's Dr. Hurst who's adamant we've a suspicious death.' Pickard made an expressive face. 'He's not long been in the village.'

'You make him sound a regular trouble-maker, Constable.'

Godwin failed to meet the other chap's eyes by studying a notice about fishing permits.

'Well, sir, it's not as if the girl had her head staved in. It looked to me as though she tripped. I can't see our old doctor making a hoo-ha about the way a body fell. He believed in letting sleeping dogs lie.' Pickard paused to swallow some tea. 'He retired and sold up.'

'Not before time, by the sound of it.'

'Er, you're fixed up at the pub, sir. Bit of luck that, for they've only the two rooms. It's a decent enough place. Landlord's wife's a good cook. Did you want to drop your bags off first?'

'Later will do. Any more tea in the pot?'

Chance held out his cup and Pickard jumped up, jolting the desk.

'You an' all?'

'Please.' Godwin followed suit.

'What can you tell us about the dead girl?'

'Young Nora Bennet, she was a house-maid.'

'Local?'

'Born here, lived with her father. Old man died, must be two year back. Worked on one of the farms.'

'Is there more family in the village?'

Constable Pickard shook his head. Several years older than the inspector, his hair was patchy dark and grey. Godwin decided he was more like a badger.

'No one left at all, that I know of. Mother died when Nora was a nipper and she was the only child. Mrs Kemp will know, that's the vicar's good lady. If I remember rightly, the girl started out at the vicarage.'

They waited for Godwin to finish jotting.

Chance fiddled with his tea-spoon. 'What about the Vernons?'

'There's only Mr. Vernon.'

'I was told there's a family and guests.'

Constable Pickard's brow unfurled like a venetian blind. 'There is a family, sir. Mr. Clifford Vernon is the owner of the house. He's the only one with that surname.'

Chance expelled a noisy breath. 'And the rest of them?'

'There's Mrs Terry, she's his sister who lives with him. A widow, very pleasant lady. Well-liked, she is, does a lot for the village.'

'Go on.'

'Then there's Miss Freda, her daughter.'

'Unmarried?'

'Yes, sir. Though the word is, she's all but spoken for. Her young man's one of the guests. A Mr. Mayhew, forget his Christian name. He came and fetched me this morning.'

'He found the body?'

'That's right, sir, the pair of them did but Miss Freda stayed behind.'

'Any more family?'

'Only Mr. Clements, Mr. Vernon's secretary, I b'lieve he's a nephew. That's all the family and they have two more guests, a married couple.'

Chance grunted. 'At least it isn't some great pile with a dozen staying.'

'Oh, no, sir, it's a comfortable old place, if you like that sort of thing. Biggest house in the village and no expense spared but it's not grand, if you know what I mean?'

'Are they a local family?'

'No, Mr. Vernon settled here about three years ago. The ladies came a while after. Mr. Vernon had been living abroad, I did hear at the time, some sort of diplomat. The old lady, who owned Holly House, left it to a distant relative who put it up for sale. Quite run down, it was but Mr. Vernon's had it put to rights.'

'Do you know anything about his other guests?'

'There's a Mr. Atherton, I believe his name's James. He's a friend of Mr. Vernon and been down several times. Drives a bottle-green Bentley. Very keen on cricket, he is, both gents are. Still a very decent bowler, he turned out for the village once.' Pickard gave a satisfied sort of nod.

Godwin followed Chance's gaze to what looked like a complete set of *Wisden* on a shelf. Not regulation in a police office.

'Contributed very handsome to the new pavilion fund too. Mrs Atherton, now, we haven't seen her before. They're recently married, an actress, they say, very smart lady.' Pickard coloured faintly. 'Saw her in church Christmas morning.'

'We'd better get moving while it's still daylight.' Chance consulted his wrist-watch and stood. 'I'll just thank Mrs Pickard for her hospitality.'

'It's no trouble, Inspector. She wouldn't hear of it.'

'Nonsense.'

'We'll be outside, sir.' Carrying his hat, Godwin led the way.

'The missus is a bit shy, like.' They waited in the wintry front garden. 'What's he like to work under, then?'

'All right. Quite decent, really.' His companion looked unconvinced. 'We shouldn't be here long. Have you any theories, being the chap on the spot?'

Pickard shoved his hands beneath his arms. 'None of it makes sense, if you ask me. Who'd want to murder a housemaid? It's not like she'd have anything to leave.'

'Could she have had a shady man-friend?' Godwin stamped his feet as he thought. 'A bad lot who arranged to meet her and quarrelled? He lost his temper and hit her?'

'Ah, you're on the wrong track there,' Pickard said.

'Come along, you two. We don't have time to idle.' Chance shut the door. 'Get the engine running, Godwin.'

'Sir.'

'Why are we on the wrong track already, Constable?'

'It's like this, sir, Nora Bennet can't have been meeting someone we don't know about. What with the snow, Holly House was sealed off last night. Snug as sardines in a tin, they were.

~

'In here, gentlemen. They're supposed to be collecting the body for the mortuary later. Only there's talk of the village being cut off and I can hardly use my surgery while it's in situ.'

'We got here from Tennysham, Doctor, though the snow's lying quite deep in places.'

'The other road out is already blocked. We had a regular blizzard on Christmas night, didn't we, Doctor? A dirty great oak came down, right across the highway. Good job no one was underneath. That'll go to the saw-mill, there's nothing like oak for fencing.'

'It's an ill wind,' Chance murmured.

Someone had closed the girl's eyes. Godwin stood next to him, intent on looking neutral. You didn't become accustomed to corpses exactly, but you learned to get past that moment when you looked.

Until last spring, he hadn't even seen a dead body. He'd almost been sick, that first time on the sea-front. Afterwards,

Sergeant Bishop had taken him aside, given him a few tips. He'd learned to breathe slowly and not disgrace himself.

Rigor had set in. He recalled what he'd been told, it began in the face and jaw, creeping down through the body. The dead girl was dressed in a jumper and skirt beneath a cheap winter coat. Her brown hair was bobbed inexpertly and she'd had a small mouth. He felt a heel for thinking Nora Bennet had been on the plump side.

Yesterday she'd had dreams.

'This is what killed her, Inspector.' Dr. Hurst indicated the wound with the edge of a clean finger-nail.

Chance looked impassively at the stray hairs stuck with dried crimson and the pale flecks.

Godwin thought about tapping his boiled egg at breakfast. That seemed a long time ago.

'What do you think did that?' Straightening up, Chance gave the doctor his full attention.

'Something hard. At first glance, the contusion appears to be the type of damage one would expect from the cranium being impacted forcefully against some solid object. Falling and banging the head against the corner of a table or a step, for instance.'

'What made you suspicious?'

'The position the body was lying in. Have you seen where she died yet?'

'No, we came to you first.'

'You'll understand better when you see the grounds. They include the site of a former religious foundation. There isn't a great deal left. I hadn't been up there myself until this morning, but there are various chunks of stone set in the grass, sections of broken columns and so forth. The young woman was found by one of these stones and the family understandably thought she'd tripped and hit her head.'

The doctor paused expectantly. In his early thirties, though his hair was already receding. He hadn't yet acquired the hearty, reassuring manner desirable in a country doctor.

'But you don't?'

'How would you expect a body to look in such a situation, Inspector?'

'I've no idea. On their face, I suppose, pitched forward?'

'Quite right, broadly speaking. I would expect the body to fall forward to the surface with the face turned slightly to one side. However, the young woman was lying on her back.'

Chance studied him. 'Look here, is that beyond doubt? There must be some leeway in how a person falls.'

Dr. Hurst stiffened. 'I realise what I'm saying makes things awkward. Nevertheless, it is my professional opinion that this death was not an accident. It's my belief that the position of the body was consistent with the victim's forehead being struck by a weapon.'

'And that fits the pattern of the wound?'

'It does, Inspector. I believe an assailant hit her with a single blow, conducted with deadly force.'

'You must have some idea of the weapon?'

For the first time, Dr. Hurst seemed uncertain. 'I dislike guessing. That's the province of whoever conducts the post-mortem.'

'Surely you can give us something to go on? A cosh, a golf-club?'

'Something with a small diameter, smooth and rounded, such as the end of a hammer. Your police-surgeon will give you an exact measurement. You can see the size of the impact for yourself.'

Chance looked at Godwin. 'Our usual question, could a woman have done it?'

His lips pursed, Hurst nodded.

'Would she have died at once?'

'Impossible to speculate. You can see the splintering of bone there. I can say with certainty that the victim was never going to recover from this assault. Whether she died instantly is another matter. It's possible she survived for a short time but she would have been rendered unconscious by the severity of the blow and beyond help. And with the freezing weather conditions,' he shrugged. 'The victim of a lesser attack would undoubtedly have perished before morning.'

'The assailant had to be facing the girl and slightly to one side? And going by the side of the brow, right-handed?'

'That's correct. He or she was also taller than the victim but that would apply to most people, as you no doubt observe.'

'Would you say the assailant had any medical knowledge?'

'I can't speculate. Oh, very well, nothing indicates that. Everyone knows that a severe blow to the temple is liable to kill. The girl would have been felled.'

'What about time of death? I know the cold makes it tough.'

'As you imply, Inspector, rigor would be slowed for several hours. It's still incomplete. I can't tell you at what hour she died. Before first light is all I'm prepared to say.'

'Thank you, Doctor.' The inspector replaced his trilby. 'If there's nothing more you can tell us, we'll be off and root around for ourselves.

'But Dr. Hurst, you saw the snow,' Pickard said. 'I'm blowed if I understand it. There were her footprints and no others until we made ours.'

~

Tate saw at a glance, as he entered the drawing-room, that much of the tea-table remained untouched. Mrs Terry had accepted a muffin from him earlier. The slices remained on her tea-plate, the hot butter congealed. She smoothed her hair, looking absently at the others. Mr. Vernon was at the French windows, polishing his spectacles as he often did when thinking.

Mrs Terry realised he was waiting. 'Perhaps you should clear away, Tate, if everyone's had sufficient.'

'Very good, madam.'

'Oh and do thank Cook for all her work. It's only that none of us have much appetite after this morning.'

'Certainly, madam. Most understandable in the circumstances.'

'I'd better come and have a word with her about dinner. It might have to be held back, only I don't want to put her out.'

'I'm sure she can cope, madam. Mrs Ruddock was glad to stay on.'

'I bet she was. Couldn't bear to miss anything.'

'Freda, please.'

'Sorry, Ma, but it's true. It's the biggest gossip she's ever heard.' Miss Freda subsided, resting her head back against the chintz.

Only the younger gentlemen had partaken freely. Mr. Mayhew, sitting on the arm of the sofa beside her, was polishing off a slice of toast, his knife smeared with Gentleman's Relish.

At the other end of the room, Gerald Clements was flicking through the weekly paper, pastry crumbs on the plate at his elbow.

'How is everyone coping, Tate?'

'Managing nicely, thank you, madam. We're all very shocked, of course.'

'If Bridget is upset, she must take things easily.'

'That's very thoughtful of you, madam, but I don't believe she and Nora were close.'

'I thought perhaps with them being of an age. I'm afraid we're all at sixes and sevens, waiting for the police. Should we offer them tea, do you think?'

Mr. Vernon turned round, saving him from having to give an opinion.

'They aren't paying a social call, Bea. They'll be here working.'

Tate moved silently around the room, collecting cups. It was a measure of Mr. Vernon's unease that he sounded testy.

Mrs Atherton was seated in the corner of the other sofa, her legs crossed elegantly. Those spike heels would play havoc with the parquet floors. She was toying with a sandwich. As he drew near, she held out the plate without looking at him.

'Not hungry, old girl? You should try to eat something. Thank you, Tate.' Mr. Atherton, standing by the piano, handed him his tea-cup. 'How's your poor head now?'

'About the same. Don't fuss, Jimmy, I'm not ill. It's only a headache and please don't call me old girl.'

'Sorry, Lois.'

'It makes me sound like a Labrador.' Her voice slid from waspish to amused.

'If poor old Digger hadn't died, we'd have found Nora sooner,' Miss Freda said.

'He was a dear old chap. Perhaps we ought to think about a dog, Lois?'

'Not in town, Jimmy. Besides, I've never had anything to do with animals.'

'You must come again in the spring.' Mr. Vernon smiled sadly in her direction. 'Freda will take you on the Downs.'

As Tate carried the tea things back to the trolley, he passed the Italian mirror and saw Mrs Atherton give the merest shudder.

'Glad to, I'll seat you on Daisy. She's as placid as they come. You took her out, didn't you, Basil?'

'I'll say, steady as a rock. Positively refused to do more than amble. Took us all afternoon to get up the hill.'

'Basil, honestly, don't exaggerate.' Miss Freda grinned at him then put a hand to her mouth. 'I actually forgot for a second, how awful. We're all sitting here, pretending it's an ordinary afternoon and it isn't. We're waiting for P.C Pickard to come back with a detective. We're all going to be questioned and one of us...'

'Hush, dear, no good will come of talking like this.' Mrs Terry leant forward, patting her hand.

'I'm sorry, Ma.'

'You don't have to keep saying sorry, dear. You've had a dreadful shock.'

'I think you're absolutely right.'

They all looked at Lois Atherton who was fitting her cigarette-holder. There was a pause while her husband snapped the flame of his lighter. 'Here we all are, passing the cake-stand, discussing the weather and avoiding the only thing on our minds. Our Yankee friends would say we're being typically British.'

'Bea's right, there's nothing to be gained by discussing it, old girl.'

'I agree.' Mr. Vernon replaced his spectacles. 'It never does to extrapolate without facts. There's clearly a lot we don't know.'

'You mean whatever your maid was up to that got her killed?'

You could have heard a pin drop. That's what he'd tell Hilda when he returned to the kitchen. Mrs Atherton didn't know when to stay quiet. And he didn't mind admitting, he was deliberately collecting the tea-things slowly.

'She wasn't a bad sort.' Mr. Clements leant forward and tossed the newspaper on a stack of *Country Life*. 'Poor kid.'

'Indeed.' Mr. Atherton looked grave. 'She can't have reached her majority.'

'She was seventeen, I think,' Mrs Terry said.

Mrs Atherton exhaled a stream of smoke. 'Does anyone know if she had a boy-friend?'

'I shouldn't think so but I suppose one doesn't really know what the house-maids do on their afternoon off. Having said that, I've seen Bridget in company with that young man who works for Mr. Murray. He keeps the village garage.'

'Tate, do you know about Nora?'

He straightened up, still holding a napkin. 'Not a great deal, Miss Freda. She did on occasion catch the bus to go to the pictures, The Elysium in Eastbourne I believe but I understood that was with Bridget.'

'Thought you mentioned they weren't close?' Basil Mayhew reached for a triangle of sandwich.'

'I beg your pardon, sir. I thought you'd finished.'

Mayhew waved the plate away. 'I'm done.'

'Bridget is a good-natured girl. Nora sometimes went to Tennysham on her afternoon off, I believe, miss.'

'Isn't that where we're all going to dine on New Year's Eve?' Inclining her head back, Mrs Atherton looked up at her husband.

'That was the plan if the road was clear, at the Channel View.'

'Sounds like a boarding-house.'

'It does rather but it's the best hotel. Very decent place, they have a good orchestra but I suppose everything's up in the air now. You must say if we're in the way, Cliff?'

'My dear fellow, absolutely not. We wouldn't hear of you leaving early, or you, Mayhew.'

'Very good of you, sir.'

'In any case, I imagine the police will want to keep us all herded together.' Mrs Atherton's voice was as dry as her preferred cocktail.

'We're about to find out,' Mr. Vernon said. 'This must be their motor-car. I'll see to them, Tate. Come with me, Clements, will you?'

'Yes, of course, sir.'

'Though what the devil I'm to say to them...'

~

'Impressive, if you like that sort of thing.' Inspector Chance's tone was intended to convey that he didn't. He had no appreciation for history, apart from a liking for old pubs. 'I wouldn't fancy the upkeep.'

'Mr. Vernon's had a lot done to it.'

'So you said. Any land with the house?' Sitting behind Godwin, he addressed the back of Pickard's head.

'Nothing to speak of, sir. There's a couple of fields the other side of the river, let for grazing.' The constable pointed across the snow-covered lawn.

They'd passed beneath the arch of the stone gatehouse that could be seen from the by-road. Clipped hollies edged the drive leading to the old house before them.

'Tudor, it is. Mr. Vernon gave a talk about the village in aid of the church. He and his sister are pally with the vicar and his good lady.'

'The church has cosied up to the big house since time immemorial.'

Long and rambling, Holly House had been extended over the centuries. The older part, with a stout, black oak door, was of pale stone. Two pairs of over-tall chimneys dominated the deep roof of brown Wealden tiles. The windows had lattice panes. The far end was built in bands of brick and flint with sash windows. A shrub with yellow starry flowers scrambled over a trellis porch.

'It isn't what I expected,' Godwin said. 'I thought Tudor meant like Hampton Court. We had a charabanc-trip there, the summer before last.'

'Never been, myself. I wouldn't mind seeing round this garden in summer. Shame they don't have the village fete here. I'd pay a shilling but we always use the vicarage garden. That winter jessamine puts mine to shame.'

'Fascinating though these reminiscences are,' Chance leant forward. 'You'll have your opportunity for a good look round the garden now, Constable. Is that Vernon on the right?'

Two men were coming out of the door, one, in a lounge suit, was in his twenties. The other, grey-haired and horn-rim spectacles, was wearing old, well-cut tweeds.

'That's him, sir. The other gentleman's his nephew.'

'Bring your measure, Godwin.'

'Got it, sir.'

Godwin pulled up as though driving an unusually slow hearse and the others came to meet them. Clambering out first, Pickard made the introductions, helmet beneath his arm.

'Good afternoon, Inspector. We're all ready for you inside. No doubt you'll want to begin by addressing everyone? Does that include our staff?'

Chance looked across to where a stone ruin dominated the view beyond a hedge. The snow was trodden and scuffed with tracks of several people coming and going.

'I'd like to see your family and guests together, sir. I'll keep it short. We'll return in the morning and interview you all individually, including the staff. But as the light is going, I'd prefer to start by seeing where the body was found.'

'Of course, I'll show you now.'

'Do you need me to accompany you?'

'You might as well, Mr. Clements. It's a pity these footprints are so trampled.'

'We were carrying the stretcher. There was no reason to watch where we trod.'

As Vernon led the way, Chance fell into step with the secretary. His turn-ups would be soaked.

'I suppose since you're here, there's no doubt it was deliberate?' Clements sounded off-hand as though it was no concern of his.

'Dr. Hurst is certain that the young woman was attacked. This is officially a murder inquiry.'

'Through here.'

They followed Vernon through an arch cut in the yew hedge. Looking back, Chance saw that the lower part of the ruin was effectively screened from the house. He doubted that anyone by the pitted walls could be seen from the first floor, possibly from the dormer windows.

'Are those windows in the roof, the servants' bedrooms?'

'Yes, that's where the maids sleep. Mr. Vernon employs two house-maids.'

'What about your room, Mr. Clements?'

'I'm at the far side, giving on to the river. Are you wondering if Nora saw something last night?'

'Just gathering information, sir.'

Vernon halted. 'I doubt she'd take it upon herself to come down if she thought she saw an intruder. We've never had any trouble here, if that's what you're thinking, Inspector? In fact, the topography makes us unusually secure.'

Clifford Vernon was one of those rangy, thin men who never get podgy in middle age. Stooped shoulders made him seem older at a glance. Tall chaps did tend to stoop. It might have been from too much study.

'I agree, sir, a burglar would have no reason to lurk out here and I dare say even they like Christmas off.'

'We get the occasional poacher hereabouts but they wouldn't cross into the grounds. There's a foot-bridge over that way behind the nave.'

Beyond the lawn, Chance could see the river curving around the gardens, about the width of a moat. That presumably had been the monks' intention, to site the priory within the protection of an ox-bow bend. The water was frozen solid and on the far bank, fields could be glimpsed beyond a straggling copse.

Chance was glad he'd worn his winter overcoat. Vernon shivered as he spoke and Pickard was hunched miserably in his uniform. Godwin, who lived at home, was warmly dressed and sporting new driving-gloves. Clements seemed a hardy type. Hands in pockets, he'd marched ahead and stood with an air of X marks the spot about him.

'This was an Augustinian house, Inspector. Not much left, as you can see but what remains is fascinating. That's what convinced me to buy the place, that and the house. This site has seen more than its fair share of history. There was a Civil War skirmish nearby. That's my subject really, and they were... forgive me, I mustn't take to my hobby-horse, eh, Gerald? Not the time.'

Clements indicated the ground. 'This is where the body was lying.'

The spot was heavily trampled. Chance looked at the sky. The day was dying. He disliked searching a place in artificial light, it never felt quite the same. Seeing Nora Bennet's room couldn't be put off, in case one of the household removed something overnight. Assuming they hadn't already but they might not have had an opportunity. They couldn't speculate in front of these two.

'Neither of you found the body, I understand?'

'That's right. My niece and Basil Mayhew, her young man, came out here after breakfast and found her. Mayhew went straight to fetch P.C Pickard and my niece ran in to tell the rest of us. Of course, we thought the poor child must have taken a tumble in the snow. Life can be appallingly fragile.'

Especially with a murderer on the premises. Chance turned to Pickard. 'What time did you log that?'

'Mr. Mayhew turned up at twenty-past ten, sir. I went right away and got the doctor and put through a call to my inspector.'

'Can you indicate the position of the body, please?'

'She was on her back with her feet about here.' Clements made a sweeping gesture. 'Wouldn't you say, sir?'

'That's right. As you can see, we assumed Nora had cracked her head on this masonry. After the Dissolution, the land was sold off to a new baronet and much of the walls were dismantled to build the house. The prior's lodging and the infirmary are lost to us. Fortunately, they left much of the nave and chancel, you see what we have scattered around. I'm sure these pieces of column are traces of the cloisters. Without the snow, you could see much of the ground-plan marked by flagstones. The position of the high altar is marked over there.'

Chance pulled a face at Godwin. Place looked like a death trap for the unwary. He took note of the distance between the ruin and where the body had lain.

'Thank you for showing us, sir. I suggest you both get back in the warm and we'll follow you shortly.'

'If you don't need us. Walk straight in when you're ready. My man will be waiting for you. Come along, Gerald.'

Chance waited until they were out of earshot, the older man picking his way over the uneven ground.

'You know these people, Constable, what do you make of it?'

'Well, sir, I've not done more than passed the time of day with any of them. Most of what I told you is village talk. I'd seen Mr. Mayhew in church but never spoken to him till this morning. I've talked to Mr. Vernon and met his friend at the cricket but I can't claim to know them well. I don't rightly know what to make of it and that's a fact.'

'Someone here knows what happened. What was Mayhew's manner like when he came to fetch you?'

'He seemed genuine, behaved as you'd expect of any gentleman. He said Miss Freda'd had a bad shock. She'd offered to show him the way to the police-house but he sent her in to tell the others and sit down. They were all of them as you'd expect, sir.'

'Do you know what line Mayhew's in, by the way?'

'Talk in the post-office is, he works in a stock-broker's office in London. He lives up there.'

'How long's he been courting the young lady of the house?'

'I couldn't say, sir, he's been down several times.'

'Godwin, any thoughts?'

'It's a shame the scene's been so trampled, sir, but we can try to rule out some of the footprints.' He produced his notebook and a carpenter's measure. 'I can't take a cast and they'll be gone if we get more snow.'

'Good chap, at least we can check everyone's shoes and we know the victim's. Nora Bennet's underneath then and look out for A.N. Other.

In the last few minutes the sky had become streaked with a vivid vermillion and the temperature was dropping. He turned to Pickard.

'Are you absolutely certain you only saw the one set of footprints this morning?'

'Yes, sir. It only struck me after the doctor examined her and said she'd been attacked. We could see the victim's footprints. There's the tracks Miss Freda and Mr. Mayhew made coming out and hurrying back. You'll see they crossed the grass a few yards over to the left of the girl's. I could see the scuffling where they knelt by the body but there weren't any other prints.'

'You did well to be observant.'

'Thank you, sir.'

They watched Godwin crouching in the snow.

'A couple of the victim's prints here, sir, facing the house.'

'As though she was watching for someone, I wonder? She was dressed for the cold, not like someone rushing out suddenly. No electric-torch with her.'

'She wouldn't have needed none. It was almost full moon last night.'

'Good point, Pickard.'

'Soon be up again, sir. What with the snow reflecting, it'd have been easy to see her way.'

'You said the gate is locked at night, so access points to the grounds are the wall either side of the gatehouse and the river. We'll take a look at the foot-bridge before we go in.'

'It's not in use, sir, I had a look this morning. Wood needs replacing, it's given way in the middle. As for the river, no one came over that way. It's iced solid but not thick enough to take a man's weight. No one's tried neither, it's smooth as glass.'

Chance gazed at the ruins, judging the distance and angles.

'I suppose the murderer could have trodden in her footprints?' Godwin's voice was doubtful. 'But it would be hard to do it without a trace.'

'I'm assuming they weren't spring heeled Jack. They managed it and I mean to find out how. We've done all we can here for the moment. Let's go in and meet the suspects.'

~

Godwin wiped his feet carefully as he followed Chance in the house. P.C Pickard had seemed quite relieved at being directed to wait in the Wolseley. He had to live among these people afterwards of course. A blank-faced butler ushered them into a great hall. He had a long red scar, almost a dent, across one side of his forehead, making his brow uneven.

The space was dominated by an oak staircase with passages leading off a gallery. A greying light was coming in from a great window with heraldic shields in the upper glass. Logs had been left to burn low in a stone fireplace, throwing out little heat and there was a tall Christmas tree. A suit of armour stood near the stairs and he noticed some weapons on the wall. An arrangement of evergreens and berries stood in a bowl on a side-table. He left his hat next to the inspector's.

They were shown into a comfortable drawing-room which seemed full of people. Someone had only recently put a match to the fire. It felt to Godwin, that the atmosphere was taut as stretched elastic.

Gerald Clements was hovering by a cabinet displaying china. An amiable-looking man, by the end window, swung round as they entered. Debonair, late forties, he studied them with interest.

The three ladies were seated. Two were by the fireplace, the older lady had some tapestry in her lap, discarded as she watched Chance. Her companion had to be the girl who'd found the body. She looked as though she'd be a good sort.

The other man had floppy, tow hair and even features, the type women find attractive. He was lighting a Sullivan, on the surface, quite at ease.

Mr. Vernon was speaking to the inspector. Godwin stood in the background and looked discreetly at the third woman. Sitting on a sofa, her bright hair lit up the far end of the room. Her made-up face was flawless. Meeting his eye, she looked amused. He looked away, with the uncomfortable feeling she could read his thoughts.

'This is Inspector Chance from Tennysham C.I.D. He's in charge of the investigation into Nora's death.' Mr. Vernon recited who they were for their benefit.

Chance gazed at them in turn. 'Please be under no illusion, ladies and gentlemen. Miss Nora Bennet was murdered last night.' There was a quick intake of breath from Mrs Terry.

'I don't propose to keep you long now. Tomorrow morning my constable and I will speak to each of you separately. For the moment, did any of you see or hear anything after you retired last night?'

There was a negative murmuring and shaking of heads. Mr. Atherton removed his hands from his pockets and spoke for them.

'We've been discussing nothing else, as you can imagine. None of us know anything that can assist you, Inspector. I'm afraid we're all baffled.'

'The best we can come up with is that the girl had taken up with a psychopathic type. You do read about such cases in the Sunday 'papers.'

Chance regarded Basil Mayhew with disfavour before looking generally. 'Which of you was the last to go to bed last night?'

Standing near the butler, Godwin saw him raise his hand to a discreet cough. Mr. Vernon answered first.

'That would be Tate here.'

'Yes, sir, I'm invariably the last to retire. That is, unless Mr. Vernon is engaged in writing late.'

'You see the house is locked up, I take it?'

'That's correct, sir, and do a last round, checking that everything's in order.'

'What time was this, last night?'

'Close to midnight, sir. The hall clock struck the quarter while I was in here. It must have been another seven or eight minutes before I retired to bed.'

Mr. Vernon broke in again. 'Tate and his wife have their rooms on the ground floor at the back of the house.'

'Was every door locked when you rose this morning?'

Something crossed the butler's face. 'The side door by the scullery was unbolted. I didn't think anything of it at the time. Sometimes Mr. Vernon will go outside early.'

'That's quite all right, Tate. You weren't to know there was anything untoward about this morning. I often take an early turn about the gardens, Inspector.'

'How many staff do you have, sir?' Chance said.

'Apart from Mr. and Mrs Tate, we have another house-maid, Bridget and Wilby, our chauffeur, he's away at present. We employ a gardener but he doesn't live in.'

'And a daily from the village,' Freda Terry said. 'Elsie Ruddock, she was here part of last evening to help in the kitchen. The vicar, Reverend Kemp and his wife came to dinner.'

'Thank you, Miss Terry. Sorry you've had such a beastly experience but I'll need to talk to you about finding the body. The morning will do.'

She nodded, her chin-length hair swinging. 'I know you have to do your job.'

'The sooner this dreadful business is cleared up, the better.' As Mrs Terry shifted, her sewing slid from her lap.

Chance gestured to Godwin. 'Take the addresses of the guests.' He turned to the lady of the house. 'We shan't be here any longer than necessary, Mrs Terry.'

'Don't be too sure, Inspector Chance,' Mrs Atherton said into the silence. It seemed to Godwin as he neared the Athertons, that she was looking directly at him. 'You might find yourselves stuck with us.'

He watched as she gestured at the window. Thin smoke spiralled from her tortoise-shell cigarette-holder. A bangle slipped down her bare wrist below the three-quarter sleeve.

Faintly visible against the darkening sky, it was starting to snow.

~

The bedroom wasn't too bad, Chance thought, apart from the cold. The mattress felt decent and there were enough blankets.

He ran through what he'd done so far. They'd stopped back at the police-house for him to put a telephone call through to London. A spot of discreet digging about the Athertons and Mayhew was in order. Routine to get some background, he'd replied when Godwin had asked. He had no suspicions of any individual yet. Nor could anyone be ruled out by infirmity.

It occurred to him, he ought to have telephoned Stella. But she'd be philosophical, having read his note and tidied the chest of drawers he'd rummaged. A policeman's lot and all that. He'd only had one more day before being back at work and there were worse places to stay than a country pub.

His window overlooked the front, where the village street was deserted. Oil-lamps glowed behind the curtains across the green. It was snowing again, drifting about the war memorial, still stark white, like an accusing finger. Chance hated to see them. Every town and village in the country was disfigured, for what? People who hadn't fought just wanted to forget. And the poor b…....s who had, didn't need reminding.

A door closed, steps hesitated on the landing before escaping downstairs. Poor old Godwin would be dreading an evening spent with him. Wondering how long to endure before he could pretend to have an early night? Dodging the awkwardness of sharing a bathroom. That one was simple, he expected first go.

His stomach rumbled, at least Godwin no longer reddened when asked a question. It hadn't passed unnoticed that he'd squirmed when Mrs Atherton smiled at him.

'Have you everything you need upstairs, Mr. Chance?'

The land-lady was waiting as he descended, her manner more pleasant than her severe face and folded arms suggested.

'Yes, thanks, Mrs Lamb, I'm very comfortable. It's good of you to put us up this week.'

Her expression softened. Couldn't be easy having policemen staying. There'd be no lock-in while they were on the premises.

'It's no trouble. The rooms are well aired and we've plenty of food in. I thought you and the other gentleman might prefer to have your supper in the back parlour. There's a good fire.'

'That's thoughtful of you.'

'Through here. You're more than welcome to drink in the bar, of course. Perhaps you'll come through in a bit but you don't want to be bothered while you dine, I'm sure.'

He smiled at her. 'Are we likely to be?'

'Well, sir, I can't deny you're the centre of attention tonight. It's only natural, people being what they are. And we've one or two regulars might come in who'd rather not catch your eye, if you take my meaning.'

Making an exasperated sound with her tongue, she drew the curtains. The small room had a gate-leg table with the cutlery laid. Godwin was warming his hands beneath the glassy stare of a stuffed fox.

'You've a colourful sign, I noticed.'

The Pheasant Inn was illustrated by a shifty rustic shoving said bird in his bag with another strutting in the foreground.

'That was painted by an artist who stayed here. Your dinner's on the way and it came from the butcher's, I'm very particular. You'll eat nothing here bought from the back door.'

'I don't doubt it, Mrs Lamb. You might reassure your regulars, I didn't come here after them.'

She gave a sharp nod. A man's name was over the door but it was clear who kept everything in order.

'D'you get many staying?'

'Not that many, Mr. Chance. A few come for the fishing and we get the odd hiker in the summer. I'll send some drinks through. If you need anything after Jean's brought your food, ring that bell on the table.'

They talked shop as they ate, keeping their voices low, despite the closed door.

'What's Sergeant Bishop going to do exactly, sir?'

'Take a gander at where the London guests live. I spoke to the Met so it's all above board. They're going to see if anything's known about them. He'll scout out the hall porter, that sort of thing, see if he can pick up any local gossip. Mayhew's rooms in Marylebone might be harder. His place may not be serviced but the Sergeant knows what to do.'

'A mansion flat in Mayfair must cost a packet.'

'It'll be out of our league, Godwin, that's for sure.'

'Seems a bit hard on Sergeant Bishop. His leave's nearly over.'

'He won't mind, he'll be glad of a break from the infant by now. Very good supper, this. I'll ask our hostess if she knew the dead girl and it might be an idea to sit in the bar, chat up the locals but we'll leave it until tomorrow. We should know a lot more by then.'

'Who do we tackle first in the morning, sir?'

Chance considered, while demolishing a hefty slice of Sussex pond pud. 'We'll play it by ear, see who we bump into. You know I like to question people when they're occupied. We'll search the bedroom again and get that suit-case open.'

'Do we force the lock?'

'If we have to but we'll have a better hunt for the key. Pass the cream, will you?'

'What do you think we'll find, sir?'

'Ask me another.' He upended the small jug. 'You tell me.'

'Family papers, I suppose. Anything she had of value. D'you think Nora was blackmailing someone, sir?'

Waving a spoon, Chance said eventually, 'ever the optimist. I can't see us being that lucky. It strikes me that if there's a blackmail victim in Holly House, they'd have been in that suit-case before us, key or no key. There's no point in murdering your tormentor if you're going to leave the evidence lying around their bedroom.'

Nodding, Godwin pushed his plate away.

'Don't look so glum. You could be right. We know little about Nora Bennet yet. It didn't seem to me there was much evidence of her personality in that room.'

'Apart from the film magazines and the chocolate.'

'Quite right, apart from those.' He thought about the large slab, half-eaten, in the bedside cupboard drawer. 'I suppose house-maids don't need to own much, living in, all-found. She had no family to store things with. We need to know a lot more about her.'

'Because victims play a part in their own murder, sir?'

'Generally, yes.'

Godwin sipped his Bass. 'They're all trying to say she must have arranged to meet a boy-friend in the grounds.'

'Of course, they are. Either that or she happened to look out of the window when Raffles was prowling and went down to tackle him.'

'Raffles was a perfect gentleman.'

'So he was. Well, you get the idea. Pin it on a mysterious stranger, nothing to do with them.'

'We know Nora didn't go to bed that night, unless she stopped to make it again. Her night-dress was folded under the pillow. If she'd arranged to meet someone she would have stayed dressed. You wouldn't risk falling asleep.'

'And if she had a secret rendezvous with someone in the house, they wouldn't risk being seen or overheard.'

Godwin nodded. 'If you were planning to kill someone, it's easier outside. The murderer couldn't risk anyone hearing and coming down before they could mingle with the others.'

'Don't forget, the murderer wanted Nora's death to look like an accident. Much easier outside but the snow complicated matters.'

'Pre-meditated, I wonder how long they had to plan it? It has to be someone under that roof, doesn't it, sir?'

Chance tapped a Players on the lid of his cigarette-case. 'Probably, though in theory, their dinner-guests could have returned. We must find out the arrangements for the gatehouse. If it's a key hanging on a hook, someone could have copied it.'

'But it was the vicar and his wife.'

He grinned, 'I agree, they're not top of the suspect list. Another thing we'll do is walk round the garden. Too late for footprints now it's snowed again. But the murderer reached the ruins by a path other than the one Miss Terry and Mayhew took.'

'I wish I could work out how the murderer got to the girl without leaving a trace.'

'Oh, I don't think there's much mystery in that. I could do it,' Chance blew a wreath of smoke. 'What I want to know is what they used to kill her.'

Two

Next Day

Jack Frost patterns had blurred the bedroom window when Chance stirred next morning. By the time Godwin joined him downstairs, there was a welcome whiff of frying bacon. They drank tea in a companionable silence while they waited. Godwin was 'mother'.

'The village is cut off, sir.' The young woman who'd served them the previous evening sounded far too cheerful for Chance's liking. 'Can't get down the hill for snow. Telephone's working, should you need it. They've been on to the post-office from the exchange. Mind your plates now, they're piping hot.'

'Will you have enough food to last?'

Godwin wasn't the only one who wondered.

'Don't you worry.' She flashed him a broad smile. 'We've plenty and the cellar's well-stocked. We wouldn't be stuck if the other road weren't blocked. They'll soon get it open. Tisn't like the north where they get properly cut off. Only we're not used to it in Sussex.'

He was lost without a newspaper. Not as lost, as he'd anticipated, without his sergeant. Young Sid was their 'flash and dabs' chap and shaping up to be a useful pair of eyes and ears. The best chance of solving Nora Bennet's murder would be while all the suspects were gathered under one roof. They would watch behaviour and collect gossip, look for discrepancies and evasions.

'Never mind your stomach, Godwin. I don't intend to be stuck here any longer than I have to. Besides, we won't be popular with the Chief Constable if we run up much of a bill.'

A couple of villagers were out and about as they left. One keen type was on a ladder, pushing a broom across his porch roof. Snow sagged precariously like icing slipping off a cake. Small kids in mittens and pixie hoods were beginning a snow-man.

The sky was muffled in barely grey. They left the Wolseley in the yard behind the pub and tramped to Holly House. It might have been a thought to bring a walking-stick.

Mrs Terry was in the hall behind Tate as they were shown in. She clutched a miniature watering-can as she greeted them. Wearing a black frock with a purple flower print, she'd made a gesture towards mourning.

'How is Miss Terry today?'

'Bearing up, it's good of you to ask.' She gave an awkward smile, revealing too much gum. 'I don't suppose any of us slept well. If you want my brother, he's in his study with Jimmy Atherton. My daughter's still at breakfast but she'll be ready to show you where she found poor Nora, when it suits you.'

'Thank you, Mrs Terry.' He glanced at Godwin who was making a meal of wiping his shoes. 'We'd like to take another look at Nora's room but might it be convenient to speak to you now?'

'By all means, I was just on my way in the library.'

'Is it all right if my constable pops upstairs?'

'Yes, certainly. Do you remember the way, young man?'

'I do, thank you, ma'am.'

'Off you go, Godwin.'

'This way, Inspector. There's never anyone in here this time of the day so we won't be disturbed.'

As they entered the library, Chance had the impression that the door at the far end of the room had just closed. They advanced and a figure stepped out from behind a book-case, making Mrs Terry start.

'Oh, it's you, Gerald, are you planning to sit in here?'

'Not at all, Bea, I thought I might have left some notes lying about.'

Clements had put on a dark tie. Chance coughed as he took in his surroundings. This end of the library was partly divided off by two book-cases, making a pleasant writing corner. He looked at the table. It held the weekly *Gazette* folded, an ink-stand and blotter.

'That's not like you, dear. I mislay things all too often, Inspector, and Gerald usually finds them for me. You shouldn't worry about work when we've guests. Clifford doesn't expect it.'

Clements smiled briefly, keeping his lips together. 'I won't be missed. Everyone's heading off to their own devices. Thought I might as well do something useful. There's some typing I can be getting on with. It won't take me long.'

'Well, it's very good of you. I hope you find your notes. Bridget knows not to move anything.'

'I've just remembered where I put them.'

'Clifford may need your help this week. There's so much to sort out. My brother wishes to provide for Nora's funeral arrangements, Inspector. There's no family and we do feel she was our responsibility.'

'An inquest will be opened as soon as possible, Mrs Terry. This weather's bound to delay matters. But the body can't be released for burial until the Coroner gives permission.'

Better not to mention the post-mortem. She looked harassed, her fading hair already coming adrift from its low knot.

'I didn't think.' Hesitating, she left it there. Her sentences tended to trail like her long silk scarf.

'I can make some preliminary enquiries, Bea.'

'Would you, Gerald? He'd be very grateful.'

'I'm glad to help. I suppose you'll want to ask me some questions, Inspector? You'll find me in my office. That's next door to Mr. Vernon's study. Turn right as you come out and head down the passage.'

'Thank you, sir. No doubt I'll get around to you after I've spoken to Mrs Terry.'

'I'll leave you to it. Don't worry, Bea.' Nodding, the secretary left.

Mrs Terry picked up the watering-can she'd set down by the window. A large, flat-leaved cactus was placed on a side-table. Some of its pink flowers had dropped on the polished surface. 'I'll leave this till later. Do sit down, Inspector Chance.'

'Thank you but please carry on, Mrs Terry.' He wandered a few feet away. The library was the province of an enthusiast, holding considerably more books than the well-appointed country home required. 'I understand Mr. Vernon writes histories?'

'That's right, he's working on a biography. He's spent much of his life abroad in the diplomatic corps but his heart always lay in England. When he gave up the service, he wanted to settle in the country, where he could enjoy the changing seasons.'

'Does your family come from Sussex?'

'No, we grew up in North London. We can get up to town for the day from here or my brother can stay at his club and visit the British Museum Library.'

'How long have you and Miss Terry been here?'

'My brother bought Holly House about three years ago. Some months later, I was widowed and we were left quite badly off, so he offered us a home with him. We've been very happy here. I suppose it won't feel the same now.'

'A house this old must have seen its share of tragedy.'

'There's been bloodshed in the distant past but that's not quite the same thing.' Her hand shook slightly as she moistened the dry soil. 'It's important not to give it much.'

'It's very colourful. How long has your nephew lived here?'

'Gerald?' She glanced up in surprise. 'Oh, I'm not his aunt. He isn't really a relation at all. Gerald is Honoria's nephew, she was my late sister-in-law. You may have noticed her portrait above the fireplace in the drawing-room. His people are dead and my brother rather took him on, put Gerald through his old college. When he came down, he didn't really settle on a career so when Clifford needed a secretary, he offered him the post.'

'Was Nora Bennet already working here when you came, Mrs Terry?'

'No, she's, she'd been here less than a year. Let me see, about ten months I think. The girl before her decided to take up factory work. Bridget came here with the Tates, as soon as my brother moved in. I believe he used an agency.'

'Constable Pickard told us that Nora was a local girl. What was she like?'

She began to collect the wrinkled flowers in her palm. 'The awful thing is one doesn't take much notice of house-maids. She did her work well as far as I'm aware. I tend to leave that sort of thing to Mrs Tate, she's cook/housekeeper.'

Chance gazed out of the window. Fresh snow had smoothed the lawn, making the day before seem like a scene in a stage play.

'How would you describe Nora?'

'She was always neat, an ordinary sort of voice with a Sussex accent. She still had some puppy fat about her middle.'

He turned to her and that seemed to do the trick.

'You mean what was she like as a person? Of course, I beg your pardon. Nora always struck me as self-possessed.'

'In what way, Mrs Terry?'

'I remember one day last summer, there was a dead rat near the back door. They nest in the out-buildings if they get a chance. It was the gardener's day off and Mrs Tate, Bridget and I didn't care to touch it. I forget where Tate was. Nora marched straight over and picked it up by the tail. She waved the body quite near Bridget's face, to show her there was nothing to be frightened of and took it to the compost heap. We daren't put poison down because we had a Labrador. Poor old boy was on his last legs then.'

'Someone always has a litter of kittens in the country.'

'Yes, we should get one. It's frightful when people drown them. I remember now, Nora grew up on one of the farms so she'd have been used to rats. Mrs Kemp, the vicar's wife can tell you more. She trained Nora from school and recommended her.'

'She and her husband came to dinner on Boxing Day?'

'That's right, after Dennis had got through all his services. It's his busiest time of year, of course.' Moving over to the fireplace, Mrs Terry tossed the dead flowers on the newly-laid coals. 'So, you see, Inspector, I do believe Nora would have come down if she saw an intruder. She wasn't a bit afraid of anything.'

~

Godwin was idling, dusting his hands at the open window when Chance reached Nora's bedroom. He'd found the back stairs and looked in the attics along the passage. The end room was used to store trunks, some papered with steamer labels. The other two were empty apart from some stacked etchings and a couple of hard chairs. The adjacent room belonged to Miss Bridget.

'Hullo, sir. No luck with the key. I've tried all the obvious places again, door-jamb, top of wardrobe, inside shoes. And I've had another look for loose floor-boards.'

'Not forgetting the chimney-breast.'

'Sergeant Bishop says it pays to be thorough.' Godwin stuffed his soiled handkerchief in his pocket.

'Quite right. Can you see where the body was lying from there?'

'No, sir, only the upper part of the ruins. The hedge blocks the view of the ground, even if you lean out.' Ducking out from the sloping ceiling, Godwin rubbed his neck, leaving a smut on his collar.

Chance took his place. 'I see what you mean, so much for their burglar theory. Mrs Terry has convinced herself the murderer was a stranger.' He recalled her shaking hand. 'Doing her best. The alternative is too dark to contemplate.'

'Do you suspect her, sir?'

'She seems a nice lady. No reason why a murderer can't be. For the moment, I'm keeping an open mind about all of them.' He eyed the scuffed, brown suit-case on the counterpane. 'Let's find out what's in here. My pen-knife should suffice.'

One last look round before he forced the lock. Despite the low cloud, there was a stronger light than the previous evening. The furnishings were decent enough for a maid's quarters, clean and neat. He guessed the bed was discarded from a better room.

The wardrobe and chest of drawers were plain deal, suitable for a servant, ditto the single easy-chair and the wash-stand. The hearth-rug on the square of carpet, curtains and cushion looked newer. There were few hiding places.

'She must have kept the key to hand.'

Not in her purse, that had been in the drawer of the bedside cupboard. She'd only had a florin, a threepenny bit and a few coppers. The poor kid didn't have a home with her own front door. She didn't need a key-ring.

The bed had a brass frame with white china knobs at the corners. They reminded him of gas mantles. 'Did you try these?'

Godwin watched as he sat on the bed and gave the nearest pair a good wrench.

'Don't stand there, try the others. It's a good hidey-hole if they unscrew.'

'When I first came in here, I had a feeling.' Godwin said, a moment later.

'What?' Chance studied him. 'Let's have it.'

'It's probably nothing.'

'Don't be shy. All detectives get feelings. Comes with the job if you're any good.'

'I had the impression someone'd been in here, sir. A woman, I mean. I thought I could smell perfume. We didn't notice it yesterday.'

Chance sniffed. 'Is that why you opened the window, to conceal the evidence?'

'Sorry, sir, I didn't think.'

'It doesn't matter. Funnily enough, I caught a mist of expensive scent in the library. Someone who didn't want to be seen speaking to Gerald Clements.'

'Mrs Atherton.' Godwin looked uncomfortable. 'I was standing next to her yesterday when her husband gave me their address. She was wearing it then.'

'Cheer up, Godwin. You're a born bloodhound. We'll find out what the lady wanted up here later.'

His gaze fell on the mantelpiece. A pair of china candlesticks, he lifted them in case the bases were hollow. A trinket box which contained the doings for sewing repairs. A wooden-cased clock, the kind that were in every home thirty years ago. He'd overwound theirs once too often. This one had stopped. Chance turned it round and opened the door in the back.

'That must be it, sir.'

Two where there should be one. 'Simple when you know. Close at hand and hidden where you'd expect to find a key.' He tossed the other one to Godwin.

'It fits all right.' He lifted the lid.

Chance poked among the contents. Nora's birth certificate was folded with her parents' black-inked death certificates and creased marriage lines.

He leafed through a few photographs. A studio pose of the parents with an infant. Another was obviously a funeral group, best dark clothes and holding flowers, like a wedding, only sombre faces. A dog-eared snap of a man in working clothes, standing by the harness of a pair of plough-horses. Love and pride shone through the grainy scene from before the War.

He would never forget the sound of a horse screaming. Far worse than a man.

'Sir?' Godwin was holding a post-office savings book. 'She didn't appear to be a blackmailer.'

He splayed the page to show the entries. At a glance, the payments were savings from wages. The balance was a meagre few pounds.

Grunting, Chance opened a leather writing-case, flipped through the contents. 'No letters kept. What's in there?' He gestured at an old shoe-box nearer Godwin.

'A few bits of jewellery. Beads, earrings, bracelet, brooches, a locket with a broken chain. Nothing valuable, I don't think. They look old-fashioned.'

'Probably the mother's.'

Standing, he looked at the bed. A few scraps were what her life boiled down to. For the first time in this case, he felt a shaft of anger. 'We'll take the savings book and papers to the police-house. Stick them in there.' He indicated the writing-case. 'Hold on.'

Someone had climbed the back stairs and was walking towards them. The footsteps stopped short. Putting his head around the door, Chance saw a girl in maid's uniform.

'Miss Bridget, I presume?'

'That's right, sir.'

'Looking for me?'

'I've popped up to change my apron, sir but Mr. Tate said if I saw you, I was to enquire if you needed anything?'

'I'd like a word as you're here. Come in when you're ready.'

'I won't be a moment, sir.'

When she joined them in her dry apron, Bridget shut the door and stood waiting.

'Do you mind speaking to us in Nora's room, Bridget?'

'No, sir.'

'Then do take the chair and be comfortable. We only want to ask you a few questions, I haven't even thought of them yet.'

She smiled tentatively back at Chance, producing dimples. Freckles speckled her snub nose. It had been a hot summer.

The girl had a good look around the small bedroom, wide-eyed at the things on the counterpane. Godwin was jammed against the wall by the pillows, Chance waiting to resume his perch by the bed-stead.

She pointed to the shoe-box lid where Godwin had spread out the contents. 'That's Miss Freda's brooch that was lost. I'd know it anywhere.'

'Which one?'

'That one, sir, the horseshoe. High and low we looked for that. In the end, Miss Freda thought she must have lost it riding. She said it was her fault for wearing it when the pin was loose. You mean to say, Nora had it all the time?' Her voice shrilled with indignation.

Fishing out the brooch, Chance showed her. 'Take a good look. It isn't possible Nora bought one like it?'

'Miss Freda will tell you, sir, but I'm sure that's hers. She was sorry to lose it. She's not a one to make a fuss and she said it wasn't worth a lot but it was to her. Her pa gave it her. She loves horses, she's gone in with her friend to run the stables.'

He raised his eyebrows at Godwin. 'Thank you, Bridget, you've been a great help.' Waiting until she sank on the edge of the chair, he resumed. 'How long have you worked here?'

'Since Mr. Vernon first came, sir. It must be three years. Before that I was parlour-maid in a big school near Horsham but I was looking out for a family post. This is easier work. I had good references.'

'I don't doubt it. Has anything else gone missing since you've been here?'

'No, sir, not that I've heard. There was never a suspicion that any of us took Miss Freda's brooch.'

'What did you think of Nora?'

'She was all right.'

'You must have chatted quite a lot, working together and up here?'

'Sometimes. If I'd known she was a thief, I'd have had nothing to do with her. I never dreamt she'd go that far.'

'Then Nora did do something she shouldn't?'

The girl hesitated, her thumb-nail picking at the side of another. 'It wasn't much.'

'I'd like to hear what she did.'

Her eyes met his. 'Sometimes she'd take people off, that's all. Like Mr. Kemp, the vicar. He's ever so nice, only he's a bit vague. She didn't mean any harm.'

That had the ring of truth, though he didn't believe it was what she'd been going to say.

Godwin shifted position. He hadn't written much down. Chance nodded at him.

'Did Nora have a boy-friend, Miss?'

She smiled back. 'Not her. When I started courting, she said I was a fool. That I'd get tied down in the village, trying to make ends meet and never know anything better. I don't know what she reckoned she wanted instead.'

'What about friends, did she ever mention anyone?'

'I think I was about the nearest. Nora never talked about anyone else. She'd go round the shops on her afternoon off but always on her own, I think. We didn't get the same hours off to go together. We went to the flicks a few times in the evening, if Mr. Tate said we could.'

There was a short silence. Godwin seemed to have exhausted himself so he took over again. 'How did Nora seem on Boxing Day?'

'How d'you mean, sir?'

'Did she behave differently in any way, excited for instance or out of sorts?'

They waited while she stared at the rug for inspiration.

'Not excited exactly.'

'Take your time.'

'Like she was pleased about something.'

'As though something nice had happened?'

'More like she knew a secret.'

'You're being a great help, Bridget. What made you think that?'

'It was a way she had of looking, sir. Like she knew something you didn't.'

'A spot of gossip, possibly?'

'Maybe... trouble for someone. She could be sharp-tongued.' She looked up at him, a picture of woe. 'It didn't mean anything. It's only the way people talk.'

'I know what you mean. We all like to let off steam. You aren't telling tales, Bridget.'

'It isn't fair to speak ill of the dead, sir. Nora could be good company.'

'I'm sure. We want to find who killed her, don't we?'

'Yes, sir. Nora noticed things about people. Like she knew when Elsie Ruddock's old man was carrying on with the new woman in the shop. And she wasn't always charitable. When it all came out, Nora said it served Elsie right. It was time she got her comeuppance.'

~

Freda Terry pulled on her kid gloves as she looked across the lawn. Sparrows were busily flitting about the hollies, dislodging puffs of snow.

'Playing croquet last summer seems like a dream now. I've become very fond of it here. The country suits me far more than industrial towns.'

'Is that where you lived before?' Chance said.

'Yes, in the Midlands. My father was a school-master but he had trouble with his nerves after the War. My mother says he never was suited to teaching. His father wanted him to go in for it.'

He nodded. There was nothing useful to say.

'We'd moved there solely because he managed to get a post. My parents had no ties to the area and then, when my father became ill again, they couldn't afford to move back south. They were trapped. My uncle was abroad and things were difficult. Eventually, father died and when my uncle came home and bought this house, he invited us here.'

And now it's spoiled, hung in the air.

'I still can't get over her hanging on to my brooch like that. Why? It wasn't even expensive but my father chose it. Nora must have heard me say so when it was lost.'

She was hatless, shaking her head set her hair swinging above her collar. 'Oh, what does it matter now? I have it back.'

'We can never know what was going through people's minds but I have to try to find out. Did you ever tell her off or do anything to get her back up?'

'Not in the least. I never particularly noticed her.'

Chance thought that may have been enough.

She looked at him. 'I'm very grateful to you for returning my brooch.'

'Not at all, it was Miss Bridget's doing. She's the one to thank.'

'I shall. Now, Inspector, you want me to show you where we found the body?'

'Is there another path to the ruins?'

She looked surprised. 'Yes, you can follow the river and come at them from the other side.'

'Let's go that way.'

Chance had been getting his bearings as they spoke. The topography had been confusing on the previous afternoon as the daylight leached away. Holly House stood in the middle of the gardens, facing south with the river looping on three sides and the drive on the right.

The open space where they stood was probably gravel. From there a few shallow steps descended to the lawn. A thick yew hedge on their left met the one they'd passed through yesterday, forming two sides of a rectangle. A line of bare trees marked the right-hand edge of the grass.

Freda set off towards the end of the left-hand hedge. She led him past the withered stalks of an herbaceous border, emerging on the river bank. The water was frozen dangerously thin.

'The path runs along here behind the hedge and the back of the ruins. It leads all the way along the bank until the river leaves the grounds. It then follows the wall to the gatehouse and picks up the river again behind the house.'

'So the path marks the boundary, more or less in an oval?'

'That's right, though my uncle owns some land on the other side.'

'Would that be where the stables are?'

'You've been asking about me. They're on the other side of the village. Why did you want to see this path?'

Their breath expelled visibly in the cold air.

'Did you notice Nora's footprints when you and Mr. Mayhew came outside yesterday?'

'Yes, I pointed them out, saying we weren't the first but we didn't think anything of it. You wanted to see how someone reached Nora without leaving tracks?'

'From what you say, someone can leave the rear of the house and pick up this path without leaving any trace at the front.'

'Yes, easily, if they want to go a longer way round. But you can't ask me to believe that my family or our friends did any such thing, Inspector. Besides, that still wouldn't explain how

Nora died. I feel as though I'm being rather shabby even talking to you like this.'

They both swung around at the sound of someone crunching towards them.

'Basil will tell you, no one had walked up to Nora before we found her. Dr. Hurst must be mistaken and he's gone too far to admit it. He's wasting your time.'

'Good morning, Inspector. You look a bit fraught, old thing.'

'Of course, I'm fraught, Basil. Wouldn't anyone be?'

'Steady on, Freddie. Perhaps you aren't up to being questioned?'

'It isn't Inspector Chance's fault, he has to do his job.'

Mayhew flung the end of his scarf over his shoulder. 'I imagine you want us to revisit the scene?'

'As you're here, sir.'

'May I leave you to it, Inspector? I can't tell you any more than Basil here. The last I saw of Nora on Boxing night was when she helped Tate serve dinner. I don't know anything and I'm getting frozen.'

'Thank you, Miss Terry.'

The two men watched her short, determined strides stamped out across the snow.

'Unlike her to get upset.'

'Murder tends to do that to people,' Chance said.

'My turn for the jolly old thumb-screws. Shall we? It's too cold to linger.'

Chance glared at Mayhew's dark, Chesterfield-clad back as they moved on, noticing a button gone from his cuff. What had P.C. Pickard said? A stock-broker's office.

'You live in London, I believe?'

'Rather. One of the hordes of humble pen-pushers, clutching bowler and rolled brolly, that's me. Monday to Friday morning, it's nose down, I'm afraid. That's why it's a relief to get invited out of town.'

Chance could see it must be. 'Do you often stay here, Mr. Mayhew?'

They'd reached the foot-bridge and a depleted wall of the old priory on their right.

'This must be the fourth or fifth time I've been down. It's better in summer, there's more going on, tennis, picnics, bathing parties.'

'So, you've met Nora Bennet several times?'

'Hang on, I wouldn't say *met*. I've passed the time of day with Tate and his missus but the girls scuttling about the place look the same in their uniform. Until she was killed, I couldn't have told you which one was her. Turns out she was the plump one.'

'You accept she was killed?'

Mayhew shrugged his elegant shoulders. Chance thought he might make a gigolo if the pen-pushing became too much.

'You and your other chap wouldn't be here otherwise. What's he up to, by the way? Not rifling through our rooms?'

'Why, should we need to, sir?'

'No offence, Inspector. I know you johnnies have your work to do.'

'My detective constable is speaking to Mrs Tate.'

Who, no doubt, spoke a lot more sense than this one, Chance thought. And he'll be warm and get a cup of tea.

'The family know perfectly well there's been some funny business, only no one wants to admit it. Lord only knows what the motive can be. I can't imagine Bea or the lovely Mrs Atherton edging along this dreary pile. She might break a finger-nail.'

Chance looked at the young man with grudging respect.

'You look surprised, Inspector. It wasn't that hard to work out. The onlooker sees more of the game, as they say at the table.'

'In that case, who would your money be on, Mr. Mayhew?'

The other man held up his hands, laughing. 'Oh, no, you can't expect me to do your job for you. I'm planning on joining the family.'

Chance eyed the uneven wall. 'Perhaps you'd show me exactly where you found the body?' Standing aside for Mayhew to go first, he followed him through a gap. A blunted stone face was high on a ledge behind them.

They crossed a vast, long space, still roughly enclosed. Chance, no church-goer, recognised it as the nave, pointed out by Clifford Vernon. They came out past the second wall, which was five or six yards at most from where the body had lain. He paid attention to a flight of steps, a dozen or so, set in the wall. The door where they led was long gone, a rusted, iron candle sconce remaining.

The blocks of stone on the ground had a fresh dusting, like icing sugar. The place where they'd stood the previous afternoon was pristine with snow.

'There are one or two pointers I could give you.' Stopping by one of the blocks, Mayhew grinned at him. 'A word to the wise and all that. Here you are, Inspector. Back at the scene of the crime.'

'Where a young woman died, quite possibly slowly.' Chance's voice was mild.

'I do see that. It's absolutely shocking. The thing is this, Vernon's only what, mid-fifties? And kept himself in good shape. I don't for a minute think he murdered the girl but I bet they won't rush to tell you he did some climbing in his young days? I'm talking about Wales and the Alps, not some mole-hill.'

'Mr. Vernon told you this?'

'It came up once in conversation. I was surprised, he seems such a bookish type. Bea did a bit herself and what's more, he used to climb with Jimmy Atherton's elder brother. That's how the two of them met, through the brother. They were in some club together.'

'Public-spirited of you to tell me.'

'I don't know if Atherton minor's done any climbing but you could look it up. They'll have a *Who's Who* in the library. He was up at Cambridge. Don't they rather go in for planting chamber pots on chimneys?'

'I wouldn't know. Do you have any athletic hobbies, Mr. Mayhew?'

He chuckled. 'Not me. I've a decent back-hand but that's all. Dancing's more my line for exercise.'

'Would you describe how the body was lying?'

'Like so, on her back, eyes open. She looked like a wax effigy, poor kid.' His face sobered momentarily.

'Is there anything else you'd like to tell me, sir?'

'Can't think of anything off-hand, Inspector. I hope you get your quarry.' Opening his cigarette-case, Mayhew looked back at him. 'Provided you don't pin it on my future fiancée.'

~

'You'll try a piece of my walnut cake with your tea?'

Thanking the cook, Godwin took the proffered plate, glad of a moment to gather his questions.

Mrs Tate watched him with the same hawk-like scrutiny he was used to from his mother.

'Absolutely delicious.' Her face said he'd got off on the right foot.

'My own recipe. I saw your boss off outside with Miss Freda. I suppose you can't say how he's getting on?'

'He wouldn't tell me what he's thinking. I'm mainly here to take notes,' he smiled apologetically.

'You'll work your way up. In the meantime, you can put down that nobody under this roof would hurt a fly.' Sighing, Mrs Tate took the chair opposite him. 'I don't know what's been going on. Something must have been and under our noses.'

They were sitting at one end of a scrubbed table. The kitchen was the first room he'd seen at Holly House where he felt at home. For all its size, it was cosy. Rows of green and white china lined the dresser, with great tureens on the bottom shelf and glass jelly moulds on the top. Copper pans and fish kettles gleamed, crinkly dark green cabbages were lying on newspaper and the aroma of hot mincemeat and pastry was seeping from the oven. Someone in the next room was running a tap.

'You'll want to know about Nora?'

'If you please, I'm interested in how you saw her. We know she grew up in Ockendon and how long she'd worked here.'

'Bridget's told us what the inspector asked. I'm not sure what I can add. Nora performed her duties adequately. We wouldn't have kept her otherwise, though we can't pick and choose like we did before the War. We don't have a large staff for the amount there is to be done here.'

A woman in a wrap-over apron poked her head round the door. 'That's the potatoes peeled, Mrs T. What are we having for afters?' Her eyes, shiny as currants, looked him over. 'You've got company. Pardon me, I'm sure.'

'You know perfectly well this young man's here, Elsie. There's nothing wrong with your ears.'

'I'm too busy working to take notice of others. Shape, is it? Only I see there's a bowl in the larder. What d'you want to go with it?'

Godwin shuddered inwardly. He'd loved shape as a boy, until he'd had his tonsils out and been given it for days. Ever since, he associated the soft slipperiness with a metallic taste, sliding over his sore throat.

'We'll open the bottled plums. You can see to them later.'

Taking this as encouragement, the woman joined them in the kitchen. The door wasn't the one by which he'd entered. Godwin assumed the uneven stone step led to a scullery.

'He'll want to question me, same as anyone else. After all, I knew Nora Bennet better than any of you. No offence, I'm sure, Mrs Tate but I remember her when she had pigtails, playing jacks in the dirt.'

Without being asked, she took the seat next to him, scraping the chair over the flags and sitting down heavily.

'Elsie Ruddock's the name, that's missus. I oblige four mornings a week as a rule and help out when Mrs Terry needs extra.'

'Mrs Ruddock has always lived in the village. She was here on the evening of Boxing Day.'

It was time he asserted himself.

'You tell that inspector of yours to watch out for himself with Mrs Atherton. She's one of them man-eaters, if you ask me. He's quite distinguished-looking for a flat-foot. Jean, that's who served you last night, said he's got very nice manners.'

Godwin discreetly leant away as she came quite close to poking him in the side.

'She said as much about you and you're more her age.'

'That's quite enough, Elsie, kindly show some respect. I won't have you speaking of Mr. Vernon's guests in that way.'

'No disrespect intended. I speak as I find. Mind if I help myself? I'm due a tea-break.'

'Fetch yourself a cup.'

He wished he was somewhere else. Waiting until Mrs Ruddock was pouring her tea, he started again.

'Did either of you ladies think Nora was different in any way on Boxing Day?'

The daily stirred her tea energetically, letting the spoon clatter in her saucer. Mrs Tate looked pained.

'She forgot the petty fours.'

'Yes, Mrs Ruddock?'

'Mr. Tate sent her back, she'd forgotten to take in your petty fours after dinner. You remember, Mrs Tate?'

'Yes, that's right. Now you mention it, Nora did seem distracted. She didn't usually need telling twice.'

'Aren't you going to write this down, then?'

Not likely, with her hanging over his shoulder. 'We find it can put witnesses off, ma'am.'

'You'll have a good memory at your age.' Mrs Ruddock drained much of her cup. 'So, did Nora. So sharp, she could cut herself.'

'How do you mean, ma'am?'

'You do have nice manners. Nora was a sly-puss. No need to look like that, Mrs Tate. I know they say not to speak ill of the dead but the police need to know what she was like. She wasn't above an uncalled-for remark when there was no one else in the room. Butter wouldn't melt in front of the family and you and your hubby.'

'What exactly did Nora do on the night she was killed?'

Fortunately, Mrs Tate managed to speak first. 'She were kept busy all evening, we all were. You'll have been told we had two extra guests, Mr. and Mrs Kemp, he's the vicar. Nora helped my husband hand round at dinner. Afterwards, we all pitched in with the clearing-up.'

'I went off after the dishes were done. That would have been about half-past nine.' Elsie Ruddock helped herself to more tea. 'Refill, Constable?'

'Not for me, thanks. Please continue, Mrs Tate.'

'When we were straight, the four of us sat down in here. I'd cut some cold meat sandwiches to keep us going. We'd had a high tea hours before and been on our feet all evening. Bill, my husband, had to listen out for the bell all the time, so we didn't bother going into our sitting-room. Bridget and Nora went up to turn down the beds, that was earlier. What else happened?'

'They were playing charades in the drawing-room when I left,' Elsie Ruddock said.

'That's right. Both the girls went up to bring some costumes down. There's some bits and pieces in one of the trunks, a fez and a coolie hat, that sort of thing. Yes, and Miss Freda sent Nora back up to fetch her Chinese dressing-gown.'

'She was talking to Mr. Clements on the landing before dinner.' Elsie Ruddock had the air of a conjuror who'd whisked away a handkerchief, revealing a rabbit. 'In the shadows.'

'What were you doing in the hall?'

'Looking round for stray glasses, Mrs Tate. You know I like to be thorough. If a job's worth doing...'

'Did you hear what they were saying?' Godwin said over her.

'Well, no, they were practically whispering. Soon as they saw me, they stepped back and he came down the stairs.'

'Can you think of anything else that might be relevant, Mrs Ruddock?'

'I can't be doing all your work for you, young man. All I can say is, my conscience is clear. Nora Bennett was alive and kicking, last I saw of her.'

'In that case, you'll want to be getting on,' Mrs Tate said. 'Those taps I mentioned.'

Godwin finished his tea while the other woman spun out finding clean rags and scouring powder.

Directly they were alone, Mrs Tate leant forward, a hollow either side of her long neck. 'I wouldn't set much store by what Mrs Ruddock says. She doesn't see as much as she thinks she does.'

'In what way, Mrs Tate?'

'Nora was sweet on Mr. Clements. Perfectly harmless, a pash as they say. It might have been Valentino, pity it wasn't. She'd be keen to do Mr. Clements's room and tidy the office for him. She'll have made some excuse to ask him something or he said something casual to her.'

'I understand.' He thought about his friend Phyllis. 'Did everyone know about this?'

'She played her cards close to her chest. I don't think anyone else noticed, apart from Mr. Clements himself. He knew all right. I've seen him look irritated but Nora had enough sense not to let it show in front of the others. I didn't even tell my husband. The truth is, I felt sorry for her. Girls feel things so deeply. Life can be sheer misery at that age.'

~

Chance felt the wet seep through his shoes as he entered the hall. It was worse when you came inside. He moved instinctively to the blazing fire, recalled his childhood in the familiar crackling. His ma would have been horrified at the waste of a fire burning in an empty room. The great space, probably used mainly for passing through, was larger than their two up two down had been.

He stepped back, looking along the panelling. The butler joined him with a quiet footfall.

'Funny thing to collect, really. Only made for one reason.' The other man fingered his brow unconsciously.

Their eyes met in understanding.

'Are those swords sharp?'

'They are, I wouldn't let the maids dust them. They need careful handling.'

'Any more weapons in the house?'

'There're two antique hand-guns and a couple of daggers in a case in the library. One of the knives was dug up in the grounds. What's left of it is past wounding anyone. The other's from Mesopotamia. Nasty curve to it. You could use that at a pinch.'

Chance looked curiously at his companion. Yesterday, he'd paid scant attention to the grave-faced, deferential butler. This was the man behind all that. A man who'd survived a trench club, if he wasn't mistaken. He knew a darned sight more than how to bow and decant port.

'What do you think's been going on here?'

'I don't know. I'd speak out if I did. I never took much notice of Nora, she was just a kid. That generation's a mystery to me but they deserve the right to get old.'

Chance nodded, acknowledging what wasn't said.

'Then you can't suggest a closer look at anyone?'

Tate hesitated. 'There's more going on than meets the eye but nothing that could be linked to Nora's death.'

'You never know, I'd like to hear all the same.'

'The wife and I are settled here.'

'Understood.'

The butler glanced behind him, studied Chance and made up his mind. 'Have you spoken to Mrs Atherton yet?'

'No, why d'you ask?'

'It's the first time she's been a guest in this house. The Athertons married in London in the autumn. Only a quick trip to a registry office, I understand, but the family went up. Mr. Vernon was best man. The guests arrived on Christmas Eve. I was present when Mr. Mayhew was introduced to the Athertons. They shook hands as strangers but he'd met the lady before, I'm certain.'

It was a butler's job to notice details and this one was no fool. 'What did you see?'

'Nothing then, it was while they were having afternoon tea. Most of them hadn't come in, Mr. Atherton was still upstairs. We always set out dishes with two choices of jam and one of honey. Mr. Mayhew ignored the jam and straight away passed

Mrs Atherton the honey for her muffins. He didn't ask her, just handed it without thinking. She thanked him and I swear she gave him the faintest warning look. It was only a tiny thing but they knew each other. It wasn't the first time they'd had tea together, I'd stake money on it.'

'Sure he wasn't at the wedding?'

'I know he wasn't. There were very few guests.'

'You'd make a good detective, Mr. Tate.'

The other man inclined his head slightly. 'It pays to keep your eyes open, as you'll know, Inspector. It can save your life.'

Chance wondered if there was something in his eyes. A policeman might well have continued in England during the War.

'Was Nora present at this tea?'

'No, Bridget was assisting me. She didn't see.'

'Did anyone else notice?'

Tate's face softened. 'Mrs Terry was the only other one there. She was too busy making them welcome.'

'Mrs Atherton's an actress, I believe?'

'That's right. Met him at a party.'

'What does her husband do?'

'Not a great deal from what I've picked up. There's family money. I think he's on one or two boards in the city and he's keen on the theatre, backs plays.'

'You're well informed. He isn't an impresario? I thought they were all fat cigars and astrakhan overcoats?'

'He's one of several investors, I believe.' Tate looked a trifle sheepish. 'A good servant is supposed to be unobtrusive to the point of invisible. You'd be surprised how people forget you're there. One of Miss Freda's chums trains race-horses. I've had one or two good tips that way.'

Chance laughed.

Tate raised his voice slightly. 'If you'd care for a cup of tea, Inspector, my wife will be glad to make you one in the kitchen. I believe your colleague is there now.'

'Maybe later, thank you, that's much appreciated. Do you know where I might find Mr. Atherton?'

Tate turned to Bridget. The house-maid was in the doorway of a room Chance hadn't seen. He glimpsed a long dining-table behind her.

'He was outside, sir, with the master. Round the back in the yard.'

'Right-oh.'

'Straight down the passage, sir.' Tate indicated with a courteous sweep of his hand. 'Kitchen door on your right and you'll see the back door ahead of you. Have you finished, Bridget?'

~

It was always interesting to see the back of a house. You'd learn more about the people who lived there behind their public façade. Chance thought about the rear of his semi. You wouldn't need Sherlock Holmes to deduce he disliked clipping privet.

The fork off the drive came out on to an area partly enclosed by well-kept outbuildings. A former stable block, converted to a garage, stood on the left. Nearby, a pump and stone trough were rimmed with snow. As he stood in the back doorway, a robin watched him. Inclined his head in a friendly nod, as if pointing out two sets of footprints.

Before he followed them, Chance peered through the upper panes in the garage doors. A four-seater Morris Cowley gleamed with polish, as though it hadn't been taken out for days. He looked at the upper storey, no condensation and the snow on the outside steps was undisturbed. They'd said the chauffeur was away.

Alongside the Morris, a modest Austin saloon had dirty streaks on its lower bodywork. Stepping inside, he flicked open the log-book beneath a pair of soft leather driving-gloves.

The third vehicle was a powder-blue Morgan, low to the ground, reminding him of a rowing-boat on wheels. The glove-box was empty, apart from a packet of Sullivans with one left. A *Daily Sketch* was untidily folded on the rear seat, *Mayhew*

Fl.4, pencilled above the banner. A ladies' cycle was propped against the end wall.

Making a mental note to put a call through to his sergeant, Chance crossed the yard to where the footprints disappeared. Watery sunlight was beginning to seep through the cloud. He could hear voices and smell pipe tobacco. His lungs ached to join in.

Clifford Vernon and James Atherton were standing beneath some tall trees. He never knew what they were. Despite keeping their leaves, they always seemed gloomy, no brightness in their green. Even dabs of snow hadn't added much cheer. The two men had their backs to him, turning as he crunched towards them.

Chance realised they'd been looking at graves. A row of small headstones, each bearing a single name, dates and a brief epitaph. He read *Devoted companion* and *Faithful friend.* More than you could say for some humans.

'Inspector Chance. I trust you're being given every assistance?' Clifford Vernon looked drawn.

'I am, thank you, sir. My constable's with Mrs Tate and I've just seen Mr. Mayhew. Has Miss Terry spoken to you?'

'Not since breakfast.'

'In that case, there's something you should know.'

'Should I make myself scarce, Inspector?'

Seen at close quarters, Atherton was several years the younger of the two. His hair, thin on top and receding, remained light-brown.

'No need, Mr. Atherton. I'd like a word with you as well.' Chance told them about the finding of Freda Terry's brooch.

'I see, thank you for telling me, Inspector.' Vernon examined the bowl of his pipe. 'It's clear we had no idea of Nora's true character.'

'Nothing else went missing since she came here?'

'Not as far as I know. No, I'm sure nothing has, so she can't have been a kleptomaniac. I can only think the girl stole on an impulse. She desired the brooch.'

'It's possible she wanted to deprive Miss Terry of something she valued.'

'Surely not? My niece is a kind young woman. She always treats the servants well.'

'Freda's kindness isn't the point, Cliff,' Atherton said quietly. 'It's what was going on in your house-maid's head.'

Vernon nodded. 'You don't waste time, Inspector. Does this discovery have a bearing on Nora's death?'

'I'm still gathering information, Mr. Vernon. It tells me something about Nora Bennet. In the light of this, can you think of anything else that might be relevant?'

'Nothing. I regret I can't assist you.'

'How about you, sir? I believe you're a regular guest here?'

Jimmy Atherton didn't reply at once. Standing with his hands in the pockets of his warm ulster, he gazed back at the house and looked embarrassed.

'I didn't really notice her much on previous visits. I've been down, what, three times this year? I know the Tates to talk to, Tate's an interesting chap. And Wilby and the gardener, he's on the village cricket team but one doesn't say much to house-maids as a rule.' He seemed to make up his mind. 'Look here, I did have to reprimand Nora. I caught her taking a liberty with my wife's things. I suppose you want chapter and verse?'

'That would be helpful, sir. When was this?'

'The afternoon of Christmas Day.'

'My dear chap, I am sorry. Did you tell Bea what was wrong?'

Chance rotated the lighter in his pocket.

'No, I didn't want to get the girl in trouble. Actually, I thought Bea might have heard us, she was on the stairs when I came out. I know it was Christmas but I had to say something. I found Nora trying on my wife's coat. At the time, I rather lost my rag but now, I wish I hadn't. She'd put up the collar, you know how women do? She was stroking the fur.'

'Can you remember exactly what happened, Mr. Atherton?'

'We'd been for a stroll in the village and I came up to change my shoes. Our door was half-open and I caught sight of her in the mirror. I suppose that proves it was on impulse.

If she was ransacking my wife's things, she'd had shut the door.'

'What must Lois think of us? Her first visit, we're practically snowed in, she's off-colour and this… awful business.'

A girl has been murdered, Chance thought. He wondered if they were trained in the diplomatic service, never to say what they meant.

'You take things to heart too much, old chap. None of this is your fault.'

'Please continue, Mr. Atherton.'

'I asked her what she thought she was doing and demanded she take it off at once. She jumped like a startled rabbit and began gabbling apologies. I watched her hang the coat in the wardrobe and she said something about never having done anything like it before, only it was so lovely. The whole business only lasted a minute.'

'Did you or your wife find anything else disturbed, then or later?'

'Not at all. My wife isn't the tidiest of women. She'll have left her things on a chair and the girl probably went to tidy them. They're all 'sisters under the skin,' aren't they? Poor little tyke would never have had good clothes.'

'Did she say anything else?'

'She begged me not to get her the sack. I said I wouldn't tell Mrs Terry this once if she never did it again. She assured me she wouldn't, started to thank me so I left her to it. No harm done, after all. I was sure she'd learned her lesson, didn't want to get a girl chucked out at Christmas for one silly mistake.'

'Did you speak to her again?'

'Not a word. She looked frightened to death when she saw me later. Just bobbed, kept her head down and went about her work.'

'Thank you for telling me this, sir. Is Mrs Atherton unwell? I haven't seen her yet.'

'She's quite up to speaking to you, Inspector. She had rather a bad head yesterday. My wife's rather sensitive. She's upset by what's happened, as we all are.'

'Lois was under the weather when she came down to breakfast yesterday,' Clifford Vernon said. 'I hope she isn't sickening for something.'

'She's never at her best in the morning. Actresses, you know.'

Jimmy Atherton had an expressive face, with a sheepish, self-deprecating manner.

Chance had met men like him, under the thumb and enjoying every minute. He didn't care for being told what to do by anyone, that included his superintendent.

'I wanted to ask you about the gatehouse, Mr. Vernon. What the arrangements are for securing it at night?'

'Wilby, my chauffeur closes the gates about dusk unless anyone's out for the evening or we've guests. Or I might stroll along myself or my niece, we're quite relaxed about it.'

'And where is the key kept?'

'In one of the gatehouse rooms. It's rather a size and saves anyone forgetting it. We don't keep that room locked but no one could enter it from outside. It's only habit that we go to the trouble. We might as easily leave them permanently open.' Mr. Vernon gestured. 'Would you care to see for yourself? The gates aren't original though they're eighteenth century. Fortunately, the previous owners had preserved some bills and other papers so we can be sure of that.'

'Thank you, I would.' Chance turned to Mr. Atherton. 'I won't need you any longer, if you're keen to get in the warm, sir.'

'I think I might, Inspector. I'll cut along then, Cliff.'

'Yes, do go in, my dear fellow. Would you tell Bea, I shan't be wanting lunch?'

'By all means.'

'I won't keep you from your meal, Mr. Vernon.' Chance checked his wrist-watch.

'Since yesterday, I don't seem to have much appetite. Shall we?'

They took a path leading behind the stable block back to the drive.

'When did your chauffeur leave, sir?'

'A week ago, Gerald took him to the station. I've let him have the whole fortnight off. His elderly mother's unwell.'

'Have you ever seen Wilby speaking to Nora?'

'Oh, I'm sure you're on the wrong track there, Inspector. I doubt they ever exchanged more than a greeting. Wilby's in his fifties, very quiet fellow.'

'Very nice Morris you have.'

'Motor-cars don't interest me but I'm aware that insurance is compulsory now. We have the requisite papers.'

'Not my department, sir.'

He spotted Godwin walking along the main drive towards them. 'There you are, Constable. Mr. Vernon is about to show us the gatehouse.'

Falling in behind them, Godwin conveyed by a grimace that he'd unearthed nothing major.

Clifford Vernon plodded with his head down, as though he found the snow interesting.

'It must be lovely here in summer, sir,' Godwin said.

Chance thought he must teach young Sid the value of an awkward silence. Wait and the suspect would fill it.

'It is indeed.' Vernon sighed. 'For all this was a house of God, this isn't the first time violent death has visited here. I'm speaking historically, you understand.'

'Did the swords in your hall come from here, sir?'

Vernon turned eagerly to Godwin, jabbing the cold air with his gone-out pipe. 'Not from this site, no. I confess I bought them at auction over the years but there was a Civil War skirmish near here. There's a map on the wall in my secretary's room. You must look at the small collection in the library, while you're here. You'll see some musket balls in the display-case. They were dug up by my gardener. We found fourteen in various sizes.'

'I'd like to see them, sir.'

'The name of Holly House is a misnomer, you know. Visitors and most of the village think it derives from these hollies along here.'

'Their trunks look old.'

'Victorian.' Vernon jabbed dismissively. 'No, *Holly* in this context has been distorted over the centuries from the original *Holy* House, d'you see?'

'That's very interesting, sir.'

'Isn't it? And here we have the priory gatehouse, virtually intact. They occasionally survive when the rest of the site was pulled down. Presumably because they were small and could be lived in. There was originally a water-mill here as well. I could show you the foundations, were it not for the snow.'

Chance gave silent thanks as their guide stopped to light his pipe. The gatehouse had a door on either side of the arch. Vernon showed them the small room to the left.

'The gate key hangs just inside the door. As you can see, we use the place as a store. The opposite room's not in use.'

Both detectives looked at the assortment of deck-chairs, croquet mallets, hoops and rolled tennis net. An archery board took up much of the space with a rack of bows against the wall. Chance regarded them thoughtfully.

'Is there anything else you wish to see, Inspector?'

'Not for the moment, thanks. We still have to speak to Mrs Atherton and Mr. Clements.'

'May I ask what happens when you've seen all of us?'

'How long are your guests staying, Mr. Vernon?'

'They leave on the second. At least, the Athertons might stay on but I understand young Mayhew must be back at his desk.'

'We shall hope to conclude our enquiries while you're all together.'

~

The public bar of the Pheasant wasn't as comfortable as Godwin had hoped, when they stepped inside. A ruddy-faced man was emptying a coal scuttle on to the fire, all but smothering the flames. Black dust and smoke spattered up the chimney. He applied a poker energetically and turned to greet them.

'Afternoon, sir. Soon be warmer now.' Wiping his hand on his trousers, he extended it to Chance. His presence was acknowledged with a nod. 'George Lamb, pleased to meet you both. I hope the wife's been looking after you.'

The inspector made polite noises and leant against the bar while the landlord filled two halves. At close quarters, Godwin realised Mr. Lamb's bright cheeks were shiny and stretched, his hands scarred. Accepting the offer of a pork pie apiece, Chance handed him a glass and looked round the room, deciding where to sit.

The few customers, who'd all gone quiet as they entered, resumed their conversations. Two old chaps were seated near the fireplace, huddled over dominoes. Two more were at the end of the bar and another was staring into his pint in the corner. Another man, short as a jockey, had slid off his stool and left while the landlord was introducing himself.

'Would you rather take your drinks through the back, where you'd be more private, like?'

Godwin saw Chance's lips twitch. The other man's manner was too eager.

'Here will do fine, Mr. Lamb. Sorry, if we're bad for custom.'

'You're both very welcome, Mr. Chance. It's a bad business brought you though.'

'You knew the dead girl, I dare say?'

'To say good mornin' to. You can't help knowing everyone in the village but we knew her old man a sight better.'

'Have one yourself, Mr. Lamb.'

'Thank you kindly, sir, I'll join you.'

'Cheers.' Chance raised his glass to them. 'Grab us a seat, will you?'

'Your very good health.'

Feeling rather a gooseberry, Godwin carried his beer to the nearest table and sat down to listen.

'Regular customer was he?'

'Lew Bennet? I'll say. Mind you, he wasn't so much before the War.'

'Ah.' The inspector glanced at the photo of a ship, framed behind the bar.

The landlord wiped a patch of bar automatically and leant closer to Chance. 'It was losing the horses did for him.' Raising his voice, 'that's right, isn't it, Arthur?'

One of the old chaps further along, nodded sagely. 'Never the same from the day they led 'em away. Used to talk about 'em in his cups.'

His profile, beneath his cap, reminded Godwin of a tortoise. Wrinkled skin, hanging from his neck, wobbled as he swallowed. His pal seemed half-asleep.

Chance looked unusually grave. 'Grim for his daughter.'

'Hard for a man to bring up a girl on his own, at the best of times.' Mr. Lamb cast a critical eye over his product and took a mouthful. 'I heard the poor sod tried to hang himself in one of the barns. I was away myself by then. Farmer found him. Course it was hushed up but telling you can't hurt him now.'

'What did he die of?'

'Pneumonia, a couple of winters back. It carried off several round here. The women tried to rally round, Mrs Kemp took the girl in but she never mixed much. Their cottage wasn't right in the village.'

'What are they saying here about Nora's death?'

'Well, sir, she's not been seen with anyone but stands to reason.' Mr. Lamb broke off as an empty tankard was pushed forward. 'Refill, Arthur? Sounds like your pies are coming.' He spoke over his shoulder, busy at the keg. 'Bound to have been a man involved somewhere. Once reporters can get here, we'll be in the *News of The World*. You can depend on it.'

'You'll be needing our rooms, then,' Chance said drily.

~

When they returned, the interior of Holly House was laced with rich meat juices and cabbage. A woman's voice came from beyond the hall, accompanied by the clatter of plates.

'That's the daily,' Godwin said.

'This way. I'd like to see the bedrooms.' Chance moved quietly up the main stairs.

The passages off the galleried landing were wider than the top floor and hung with prints. A door was open outwards and someone behind it. As they drew near, a short figure stepped out, arms full of folded towels.

'Ah, Miss Bridget. Which is Mrs Atherton's room?'

'Along here, sir but they're all downstairs having coffee.'

'Splendid. Don't just stand there, Godwin. Assist the young lady.'

'I'll take those for you, miss.'

'Lead on, Bridget.' Chance gave her his best smile. 'Policemen are only human, you know. Keen to get a peek at how the other half lives.'

The dimples appeared again. 'This is the master's room, sir.'

While she busied herself, Chance gave the room a swift appraisal. No burglar could have sized up the fittings faster. Leather slippers placed parallel on the rug, beside a great mahogany half-tester. Bed-time reading, something battered, the window overlooked the front.

'This is the Athertons, sir, the main guest-room.'

'Very nice,' he lied absently.

Not nearly so masculine. Vaguely Chinese with a bird-patterned paper and ghastly vases. Godwin looked embarrassed as Bridget reached for a towel from the pile he held.

An eau-de-nil silk robe was flung over a chaise-longue, sash draped on the carpet. Chance watched the girl hang it in the corner wardrobe. A dressing-table was littered with expensive pots of face cream, a drum of powder, brushes, glass-stoppered scent bottle, a packet of sleeping-powders, an eye-mask and an ash-tray. Jimmy Atherton had staked his modest territory with a pair of horn-backed hair-brushes on a chest of drawers.

'What else did Nora get up to, Bridget?'

'I'm not sure what you mean, sir?' She eyed him, wanting to edge past.

'This morning, when you were telling us about her, you hesitated and kept something back. Did she search through people's things?'

'She wasn't above peeping. Like you said, sir, it's human nature and guests like Mrs Atherton have such pretty things. I wouldn't do it but you couldn't always stop Nora.'

'Did she ever tell you she'd taken anything or read letters, perhaps?'

Godwin looked away towards the window. The girl's mouth had gone round as a saucer.

'Oh, no, sir, I swear she never said anything like that. But if Miss Freda'd bought something new, Nora might hold it up against herself. She wasn't above trying a spot of cream and once she dabbed a guest's scent behind her ears. I begged her not to, in case they noticed.'

'And you aren't hiding anything else? Because someone murdered Nora. This is no time to worry about her reputation.'

'I'm not, sir, on the Bible.'

He treated her to his stern look. 'Good girl. Which is Mr. Clements' room?'

'He sleeps down the other end, sir. I'll show you.'

~

While they waited for Mrs Atherton to join them in the library, Chance pulled a *Who's Who* from the shelves.

'Let's see if they're there. A former diplomat should be. Yes, here we are.' He read extracts aloud. 'Educated Cambridge, a rowing blue, no less, cricket, list of works published, de da de da. James Peregrine Atherton, poor swine. Interests, theatre, cricket, various clubs, usual dull stuff.'

Replacing the volume, he wandered over to where Godwin was examining a glass display-table.

'This reminds me of Kim's game, sir. You know, memorise twenty objects on a tray?'

Chance slipped the catch and examined a couple of items, reading the labels. 'If our victim had been stabbed or run through, we'd be spoilt for choice in this house.'

'At least you worked out where the murderer stood without leaving footprints, sir.'

Chance held up a hand, motioning silence. The door opened and Mrs Lois Atherton stood poised on the threshold, one hand lightly on the door-knob. *Enter, stage left, from the wings*, he thought. It was decidedly an entrance.

'You wanted to see me, Inspector?'

'Thank you, Mrs Atherton. We shouldn't keep you long from your friends. Please, do make yourself comfortable.'

He waited until she'd taken an arm-chair before sitting opposite. Godwin took the hard chair he'd fetched from the table.

'I'm in no hurry to get back.' Arranging her skirt, she sat back with legs crossed, a hint of mischief in her face. 'There's only so much interest I can fake in hearing about people I've never met. I don't play bridge and shamefully, I've never done any good works.'

'This is your first visit here, I believe?'

'Yes, I'm here on sufferance, Inspector, because I married their friend.'

'I'm sure that's not true, Mrs Atherton. The family seem like very decent people.'

'Oh, they are, too decent to say what they think. They see me as a gold-digger. Their dear old chum was a confirmed bachelor until someone brought him to the second-rate play I was in and I used my wicked wiles to trap him.'

'I've never been quite sure what wiles are.'

'I didn't trap him, whatever they think.' Her voice was defiant. 'I love my husband, Inspector. I don't deny I was sick of miserable digs and ordering the cheapest snack in Lyons'. It's marvellous to let rip with money and be taken care of but I'd feel the same if Jimmy were penniless.'

Chance found he believed her.

'Had you met anyone in this house before, apart from Mr. Vernon, his sister and his niece?'

'No, I hardly know Sussex. A day-trip to Brighton like most Londoners and I once had a week in rep in Worthing. After this stay, I'm not inclined to come back.'

'I noticed you'd been talking to Mr. Clements in here this morning. Was that about anything in particular?'

The lady raised her eyebrows. 'I'm not sure that's any of your business, is it?'

'Detectives are incurably nosy, it goes with the job. A young girl has been murdered and I'm afraid that gives us the right to ask all kinds of intrusive questions until we find the perpetrator.'

Her face sobered and she sat forward. 'I was looking for my husband. Nothing else. I think Gerald Clements is a phony. He spends all his time making up to his uncle and aunt, making himself indispensable. He acts like a prig but he doesn't *feel* like one. I assume you're getting us to dish the dirt about one another, so there's some for you, Inspector. Do make sure you take it all down.'

She flashed Godwin a smile. He looked uncomfortable.

'All contributions gratefully received,' Chance said. 'I'd rather like to smoke. How about you?'

'Please.'

As he reached inside his jacket, Mrs Atherton stood in one graceful movement and handed him the silver box on the mantelpiece. 'Why not try these?'

'Thanks.'

'Constable?'

'Not for me, thank you, ma'am.'

Chance lit her cigarette first, when she was seated. Seen this close, she was starting to line about her eyes. Good bone structure would always serve her well and her white-blonde waves were almost too perfect. He guessed late thirties. The one ageing thing that face-paint couldn't conceal was experience. Those blue eyes had seen too much.

'No cigarette-holder this afternoon?'

She grinned suddenly. 'It's a perfect nuisance but looks the part.'

Amused, Chance savoured the expensive taste on his throat. A Turkish blend. He removed a loose shred of tobacco.

'You don't look so formidable when you smile, Inspector.'

'You might want to revise that in a moment, Mrs Atherton. Are you quite sure you didn't know any of the guests previously?'

Filling her lungs, she exhaled slowly. He wondered what non-smokers do when they want time to think.

'Very well. I could spin this out but I'm sure your time is too valuable to waste, even if mine isn't. Cards face up, then. You've obviously found out I knew Basil Mayhew. Might I ask who told you?'

'Sorry, policemen are like doctors and journalists.'

'Was it my husband?'

'No. One of the staff noticed something.'

'The girl who was killed?'

Chance shook his head.

Mrs Atherton stared thoughtfully at him. 'Look, I don't want you to get the wrong idea. Jimmy isn't insanely jealous or anything like that. He understands I had a life before we met. It was a shock to see Basil here and I pretended we were strangers instinctively. Now it's too late to tell Jimmy we knew each other. Do you understand?'

'We do.'

She turned to include Godwin in her look and seemed satisfied. 'I hadn't seen him since last year. Someone brought him back-stage to a sort of dressing-room party and we clicked.' Her chin came up. 'I knew him well for a time. Then these things tail off with no bad feeling on either side.'

Chance thought it all sounded rather sad.

'We don't enjoy being intrusive. It's just that when someone's lied to us or been evasive, two stories don't agree, we need to clear that out of the way.'

'And hope at the end, you're left with the answer?'

'Something like that.'

'I truly don't think Basil is your man. He's weak, he likes fun and an easy life but he isn't vicious.'

'I understand he's nearly engaged, as it were, to Miss Terry. What if Nora was blackmailing him? Might Miss Terry break it off, if she knew of your relationship?'

She twisted out her cigarette. 'I don't know her well enough to say. She's awfully far gone on him. Someone here murdered the girl. None of them want to admit it. Basil, Jimmy and I are outsiders. We didn't know Nora. I'd look to something that's been going on here.'

'Your husband had met Nora on several visits,' Chance said mildly, 'for the sake of argument.'

'She was a house-maid, that's hardly meeting someone.'

'What did you make of her?'

'I didn't see much of her. We only arrived on Christmas Eve. The other girl, Bridget, served at tea and dinner that night.'

'Did you happen to see anyone else talking to Nora? Does anything strike you in hindsight?'

'She was smitten with Gerald, I noticed that. I don't think the rest of them knew.'

'Including Mr. Clements?'

'He didn't treat Nora any differently from the other staff. Look, Inspector, I can't tell you anything to help you. I'm counting the hours until we can leave here.'

'Does Mr. Atherton feel the same way?'

'He's concerned about his friends, anxious to see this cleared up. Everyone's under a cloud until you do but we don't have to live in a village.'

'Why were you in Nora's room this morning?'

There was a flash of reaction in her eyes but her voice was as unconcerned as his.

'I wasn't, at least, not intentionally. I was looking for the other girl. A hem's come down on one of my frocks and Mrs Terry said Bridget would mend it for me. You seem remarkably well-informed, Inspector Chance.'

'I'm sure we all agree, the sooner this is cleared up the better.'

She shivered. 'It isn't pleasant being stuck here and wondering who. Had you heard the old priory is supposed to be haunted?'

'No, I hadn't.'

'There is something you've missed? Some monk who kicked over the traces. He was supposedly killed by a chunk of stone falling from the wall and it was said to be a judgement. People claim they've seen a black-robed figure walking by the wall. Utter rot, of course. Have you finished with me?'

'Yes, I think we have, Mrs Atherton. Would you mind asking Mr. Clements to come and have a word?'

'With pleasure.'

Once again, she posed by the door. 'Ghosts don't scare me. You hear the stories all the time in old theatres. It's what the smiling person next to you might be like inside. That's what frightens me.'

As soon as they were alone, Chance stretched and wandered to the window.

'A shrewd lady. What d'you make of them, Godwin?'

'On the face of it, sir, it's hard to see any of them as a murderer.'

Chance grunted. 'I learnt long ago, there's no such thing as behaving suspiciously. Every bally suspect will lie or act shiftily or fall over themselves to be too helpful and they're the worst ones. That's all perfectly normal behaviour. Let's narrow it down. Is there anyone we can eliminate?'

'The married couples? Unless two were in it together, the butler and Mrs Tate alibi each other and so do the Athertons. We saw they're sharing a bedroom.'

'Maybe but one of them could have slept through the other creeping out. Did you notice, Mrs Atherton, for instance, had sleeping-powders on her dressing-table?'

'I didn't, sir. Does that mean we can't rule anyone out?'

'Your Mrs Ruddock. We know she left and couldn't get back in again. Not unless she lifted the key to copy. And we'll exempt the vicarage. The murder took place after midnight. An appointment was made between Nora Bennet and her killer. They'd have waited an hour or more for the household to settle. Anyone of them *could* have done it. I'm inclined to rule out one or two... Chance paused, hearing a door close. 'He's coming, back to business.'

'Good afternoon, Inspector.'

Gerald Clements took the arm-chair, appearing composed. 'I don't quite know how I can assist you but do fire away. I gather I'm the last to be questioned.'

'You mustn't feel left out, Mr. Clements. We did speak yesterday and see you this morning. Have you had any further thoughts regarding Nora's death?'

'My views haven't changed. It's ridiculous to suppose anyone in this household murdered one of the servants. And it's equally insane to suggest one of my uncle's guests murdered the girl. Surely you can see that, Inspector?'

'I can see it seems unlikely, Mr. Clements. Nevertheless, a young girl is dead and someone is responsible. I intend to see they answer for it.'

Clements brushed an invisible speck from his trouser leg. 'I suppose we can look forward to detectives from Scotland Yard doing all this again when the roads are clear?'

Chance exchanged a look with Godwin. 'I think the Chief Constable will give us more than twenty-four hours to make an arrest.'

'As a friend of the family, he'll want this handled quickly and discreetly. I should question Dr. Hurst again, if I were you. You don't want to get egg on your face because he's made a mistake and won't own up.'

'I understand you aren't actually a member of the family, Mr. Clements?'

The young man's face darkened. 'I don't see what that's got to do with anything. Clifford Vernon is my uncle by marriage.'

'Were you on friendly terms with Nora?'

'Certainly not. One doesn't befriend servants.'

'You didn't speak to her on Boxing night?'

'Naturally, I thanked her if need be.'

Chance folded his arms.

An exaggerated sigh and Clements continued. 'She spoke to me on the landing. Old mother Ruddock was skulking in the hall. She told you, I suppose?'

'We'd like to hear what Nora said, if you could cast your mind back?'

'Sorry to disappoint you, Inspector. The Kemps had just arrived. She made some girlish remark about the ladies in their evening-dress. Why she said it to me, I can't begin to imagine. Something about Marjorie Kemp getting out her garnets and Lois Atherton in her diamonds. I think she meant it to sound disparaging but she was clearly eaten up with envy.'

Three

A chap on a tractor rumbled carefully past them as they reached the village green. Chance stopped on the corner. 'You might be able to drive us tomorrow. I'll have had enough of trudging along like Good King Wenceslas and his page.'

'He's having to take it slowly.'

'Unlike us. This is where we part company for the moment.'

Godwin looked at him in surprise. 'What do you want me to do, sir?'

'Cut along to the police-house and see if Sergeant Bishop's left a message yet. If he has, I want you to get hold of him at his daughter's. Ask him if he can find out one more thing for me. It's all here.' Chance handed him a page torn from his note-book. 'Otherwise, ask him when he calls.'

'Will do, sir.' Reading the sentence, he looked up sharply. 'Does this mean...?'

'Too soon to say. Just something I'm curious about.'

'He might have left a message and not be back at his daughter's yet.'

'Don't make difficulties. You can type up your notes while you're waiting. I'm calling on the vicar so I'll see you later.'

Several points had struck him during the day but once he latched on to something, it was hard to get out of his head and he'd been wrong before. If he was on the right lines, he needed evidence and he didn't know how Nora found out. Only the murderer could tell him that.

The old church had a short bell-tower faced with wooden slats, not unlike that on an infant school. As he walked up the drive, Chance thought he wouldn't fancy living with head-stones over the low wall. Not exactly cheerful, being reminded of the grim reaper every time you opened your curtains. He supposed it was different for vicars.

The vicarage reminded him of a dolls' house. Dead-looking rose bushes poked out of the snow and he could make out the edge of a carriage sweep. Chance pushed his cigarette-end into the snow and used the boot-scraper by the front door. He raised his hat at the young house-maid who answered.

Shown into the hall, he waited with some amusement for a reply to the breathless, 'Please, ma'am, it's the police. I told him vicar's gone out but he said you'll do.'

Mrs Kemp was small with grey hair wound into bell-pushes over her ears. She had an eye-reaching smile.

'Do sit down, Inspector. I was about to order some tea if you'd care to join me? Now, are you allergic to fur? I know some people are and not everyone likes cats.'

One green eye opened in what could have passed in a dim light for a black cushion. Paws stretched and the eye shut again as Chance took the other corner of the sofa.

He admitted to not minding fur. Provided it wasn't all over his trousers.

'Ah, you're a fellow cat-lover. They can always tell. Jeremiah would stalk off in a huff if you weren't sympathetic to him.'

He ignored Jeremiah as she remarked on the seasonal weather, until the girl returned with a tea-tray.

Chance realised how tired he was as Mrs Kemp poured his tea. They were in a pleasant room, made cheerful with wine-red velvet curtains, echoing the holly along the mantelpiece. The sofa was deep and comfortable. He'd been watchful for hours and now out of the cold, soothed by the firelight, it would be easy to nod off.

'I'm sorry my husband isn't here to meet you, Inspector. He's gone to sit with a sick parishioner. I doubt he could help you though. He had little to do with Nora when she was here.'

'I understand you gave Nora her first job?'

'That's right. We try to take in local girls and I do my best to train them and place them in better positions. I gave Nora a reference for Mrs Terry after she'd been with us about eighteen months.'

'I've been at Holly House most of the day.' He considered how to continue as he drank some tea. 'I'm sorry to tell you this, Mrs Kemp.' He related how Bridget found Freda Terry's brooch.

'Dear me. Then I'm very much at fault for recommending Nora. She wasn't popular with Cook or the other maid we had at the time. An awkward child in some ways but no badness in her. She was more than satisfactory in her work and I would never have thought her a thief.'

'Why wasn't she liked by your other staff?'

She gazed into the flames. 'Some people don't have the knack of making themselves liked. I'd known Nora as a village child all her life. She was one of those girls who never get picked for skipping-games. They learn that they don't fit in and often acquire a prickly manner in defence. She had no mother or brothers and sisters to rub along with.'

'I've been told she spoke disparagingly about the other young women in the village. She wanted more from life.'

'That can be unwise.' Mrs Kemp set down her cup. You know, she was always kind to Jeremiah when she lived here. That counts for a lot with me.'

He watched the moggy's eyes become slits at his name. 'I'm sure you and Reverend Kemp were very kind to her.'

'Nonsense.' Her voice was brisk. 'We only did what anyone in our position would. Nora needed a place and we needed a house-maid.'

'You must have still seen her frequently. Were you aware of any change in her?'

'No, Inspector. I did see Nora and ask how she was. Beatrice Terry is a dear friend and I'm often at Holly House or she here. But Nora wouldn't confide in me.'

'Did you see her on Boxing night?'

'Yes, she took our things when Tate showed us in and she was serving throughout dinner. She seemed perfectly happy. At one time, I noticed she was smiling to herself.'

'When was this, Mrs Kemp?'

'When the men were at their port. We were in the drawing-room and Nora was serving sherry. At least, Bea and I had sherry. Freda and Lois Atherton were drinking cocktails. Mrs Atherton was making them herself. I don't believe I've ever met an actress before, though I knew her husband has some connection with the theatre. She looked so glamorous with that pale colouring and her diamonds. She was wearing a beautiful midnight-blue, beaded gown.'

'Someone else mentioned the diamonds.' Chance helped himself to a biscuit.

'The necklace belonged to Jimmy's mother. He gave his wife matching earrings on their wedding day and a diamond comb for Christmas.'

'Is this Mr. Atherton's second marriage?'

'No, Inspector. I can see why you might assume that. Jimmy's never married until now, though he's popular with everyone. They met at a party and wed within a couple of months. Eyebrows were raised, of course but it isn't unknown. Young people think only they feel romantic love and the middle-aged have no strong feelings.'

Chance smiled at her. 'The young think no one old ever experienced anything in the way they do.'

'That's very true. I like Lois Atherton. She's another one who's prickly. Fitting in Jimmy's circle can't be easy for her, apart from his friends in the theatrical world. People will say she married him for his money, particularly as I gather she wasn't at the top of her profession.'

'You don't believe that's true?'

She shook her head slightly. 'Do have some more shortbread. You need sustenance in your work, Inspector.'

'Thank you, they're looking after us very well at The Pheasant. Had you met Basil Mayhew previously?'

'Yes, several times. We came to dinner when he was staying with Clifford in the summer and saw him at a tennis-party and the village cricket match. He accompanied Freda yesterday when she came to tell us Nora was dead. Bea had wondered if Basil was going to propose to Freda this week, before this tragedy. Not the right time now he'll be staying on for the inquest.'

'Yes, he'll be required to give evidence as he found the body with Miss Terry.'

'You look surprised, Inspector Chance. A vicar's wife soon learns to be practical. Her husband's mind is usually on more spiritual matters.'

Again a twinkle in her eyes. He suspected many villagers had sat where he was while Mrs Kemp listened.

For once, he declined more tea. 'I expect you know Gerald Clements fairly well?'

'We're often at the same gathering but I don't feel I know him well. I get the impression it's dull for him down here. He gets up to town quite a lot.'

'Are he and Mr. Mayhew friends?'

'They're on good terms on the surface. They play billiards, that sort of thing but friends? No, I think Basil Mayhew doesn't take much notice of Gerald and Gerald dislikes him. I believe that's what you're really asking, Inspector?'

'Thank you for being so frank with me, Mrs Kemp.'

'I hope you'll believe I'm usually more discreet but these are mercifully rare circumstances.'

'Of course. I'm here for a short time and if I'm to find out the truth, I need people to talk openly to me.'

'A difficult responsibility. We shall owe you and your colleague a great debt if you can end this tragedy. Nora had scarcely begun her life. The worst outcome will be if the murderer is never found.'

He was horrified to see her eyes were shiny. Chance stood and picked up his trilby.

As he passed through the brick gate-posts, he was still thinking over their conversation. The sun had gone in. The houses opposite were masked by laurels and old walls. No birds around, the quiet lane seemed to belong to the dead.

Chance rather thought he'd just spoken to the only person who mourned Nora Bennet. He supposed the girl's body would lie there over the wall. She'd never left Ockendon and it was too late now.

~

Godwin let him in, looking pleased with himself. 'I've found something you should see, sir.'

'Let me get in the door.' Removing his muffler, Chance tossed it on a chair with his other things. P.C. Pickard's office didn't run to a coat-stand.

'Where's the fire?'

Godwin picked up a sheet of writing-paper by its edge and handed it to him.

He gave a low whistle. 'Where'd you find this?'

'In Nora's writing-case. I was going through her papers again and noticed the lining's come away at one edge. This was slid inside. At first I thought it was stiffening.'

'And you checked. Well done, Godwin, I'm impressed.'

'Thanks, sir.' Godwin held open his note-book. I've compared it against Mr. Atherton's and Mr. Mayhew's hand. They wrote down their addresses for me yesterday.'

They studied a selection of Clifford Vernon's signature with minor variations. The pen-strokes grew more confident down the page.

'I'm no handwriting expert but I'd rule them out. How about you?'

'I think this has to be Gerald Clements' work, sir. Surely it wasn't Mrs Terry or Freda?'

'Not a female fist, I think. There's the Tates but my money's on Clements.'

'It gives him a motive. This could send him to prison.'

'Only if Clifford Vernon pressed charges. If we confront Clements with this, he'll say as Vernon's secretary, he's authorised to sign letters on his behalf. Vernon will back him up for the sake of his dead wife's memory or whatever. The whole affair will be hushed up. That lot all stick together.'

'I hadn't thought of that.'

'Cheer up, Godwin. You look as though you've lost ten bob and found a tanner. It's my job to be jaundiced.'

'This proves Nora was a blackmailer.'

'I wonder where she pinched it from? She probably rooted around when she was cleaning his room. Did he know she had it? If Mrs Tate was right about Nora being keen on Clements, she may not have been after money.'

Godwin coloured. 'Surely not, sir?'

'Not that,' Chance was impatient. 'It's power over someone. A servant doesn't get to feel much power. They're on the receiving end. You know she may have taken this to protect him. Perhaps he's a young idiot who left it lying around?'

'Do you want me to finger-print it, sir? I've been careful how I handled it.'

'No point. We'll wave it at him in the morning and get him to cave in.'

'Does this mean Clements is our man?'

Chance looked through the window. 'Here comes Pickard. Good, his missus'll put the kettle on. They serve Earl Grey up at the vicarage. I can put up with it, if I must. But I'd rather my tea didn't taste as if someone spilt scent in it. Has Sergeant Bishop been in touch?'

'Yes, sir, I was coming to that. I spoke to him myself.'

'Good, what did he have to say?'

'He went to the addresses. He said, no luck at the Athertons' flat. They live in a block with a hall porter who wouldn't give him the time of day. But a char-lady let him in at Mayhew's building. She does for all the tenants and was only too pleased to chat about the young man upstairs. Apparently, he has a procession of lady-friends visiting and has been known to forget to leave her money. But he gives her a fancy box of chocolates now and then and has ever such lovely manners.'

Chance grinned, he could hear his sergeant's turn of phrase. 'You passed on my message?'

'Yes, sir. The Sarge said he'll see what he can find but if he doesn't ring back by six, he's drawn a blank. Oh and you owe him a pint and some shoe leather.'

The door opened with a thud.

'All right if I join you, sir?'

'Come in, Constable. It's your office.' Chance lowered his feet.

'The wife thought you might like a cuppa.'

'How very kind. Don't just sit there, Godwin, shift that typewriter.'

When they were settled, Pickard cleared his throat. 'Mind if I ask how you're getting on, sir?'

'It's a reasonable question. It's your patch.' Chance drank some tea. 'This is more like it, very decent of Mrs Pickard to look after us. How would you say it's going, Godwin?'

'We've finished interviewing everyone at the house and the Inspector's been to the vicarage.'

'Does that mean you'll be off tomorrow, like? Only the other road should be open. Snow's packed nice and firm. They're clearing the tree this afternoon. The Tennysham road'll be treacherous if it freezes again. I wouldn't try going up on the Downs but you should be able to get the long way round and sleep in your own beds tomorrow night.'

'Anyone would think you wanted to get rid of us, Constable.'

'I'm sure he's only thinking of us, sir. I'll be glad to get home.'

'I was wondering if the Chief Constable will be calling in Scotland Yard, sir?' Pickard crammed his mouth with some of his wife's cake.

'You're not the first person who's wondered that.'

'Have you worked out how the murderer did it without leaving footprints.'

'Godwin?'

'They approached indirectly. Along the path by the river, through the ruins, then made their way along the outside wall to get close enough. The inspector got on to it right away.'

Pickard scratched his nose. 'Taking a risk, weren't they? What if they fell?'

'Too low to fall.' Chance stretched out his hands to the inadequate paraffin heater. 'Those walls have plenty of ledges. With so many uneven stones, there are hand and footholds everywhere. The snow's barely settled on them and you could move along as little as a foot above the ground, quite easily. Anyone who wasn't elderly or infirm could do it.'

'But why go to that trouble in the first place?'

'There's only one logical reason. To make Nora Bennet's death look like an accident. If I were the murderer I'd think to myself, if it doesn't come off, no harm done. But if there's no sign anyone else was present, there's a jolly good chance the police will think she slipped and cracked her head. After all, the snow makes a fall more feasible.'

'I still don't see how she was murdered.' Constable Pickard had a moving lump in his cheek as he worked his tongue round his mouth.

Chance supposed he was chasing a raisin round his dentures.

'There are two places where someone could stand and aim something. An aperture that's a sort of empty window sill but even better, there's a set of steps on the wall that lead nowhere. You could stand there comfortably and raise your arm. Nobody would have reason to go over there and search for footprints.'

'But if you're right, sir, how did they kill her?'

'With a missile. It was almost full moon, remember? You're the one who said it was as bright as day. She was struck with something that would lie unnoticed on the snow, if it didn't sink in.'

Pickard's Adam's apple wobbled. 'I still don't get it.'

'I think the murderer killed Nora with a catapult.'

Godwin thumped the desk. 'The one in the curio case in the library.'

'That's the one. Old but perfectly serviceable, I tested the elastic earlier. Well-made too, nice leather sling. Won't take finger-prints though, will it?'

'Not the wood, sir. Maybe get a partial on the leather, if they didn't wear gloves.'

Pickard looked from one to the other. 'You mean she was killed by a stone?'

'Not quite,' Chance said. 'Something better. You know, it's hard to get the right stone for accuracy. They mustn't be weighted on one side or too irregular in shape. But get it right and they're lethal.' He grinned at them. 'I know this from hitting tins, you understand. I never aimed at a dumb animal. At other boys, of course, we were bloodthirsty little blighters. Lucky none of us lost an eye.'

'If it wasn't a stone, then what was it, sir?'

Ignoring Pickard, Chance looked at Godwin. 'You've seen something near identical, several of them.'

Godwin blinked several times, a slow smile spread over his face. 'The musket balls.'

'Well done. When Clifford Vernon was taking us to the gatehouse, he was telling you about Holly House. Contrary to popular belief, I was listening. He said there were fourteen musket balls in the display-case. Earlier this afternoon, there were eleven.'

'But the murderer wouldn't have had time for three attempts,' Pickard said. 'She wouldn't stand still while someone took pot-shots at her.'

Chance looked at the ceiling. 'Do it right and you'd only need one go. But if I were the murderer, I'd take spares in case I dropped one while I was getting in position.'

'No point trying the case for prints,' Godwin said. 'Bridget will have dusted the library since or Mrs Ruddock. Anyway, the murderer would make sure they openly leant on the glass.'

'Not to worry.'

Pickard felt the weight of the tea-pot. 'What if they'd missed? You'd have to be sure she was dead.'

'If she was unconscious, she'd have died of the cold by morning.' Godwin watched Chance's face for confirmation. 'And the murderer must have had a back-up plan to stab her or bash her over the head. Do you agree, sir?'

'I'd nip over and strangle her, myself.'

'But if it could be passed off as a tragic accident, the murderer would be safe. Whoever did it must have been confident.'

'Or desperate,' Chance said.

'It doesn't feel like something planned for weeks, more cobbled together.'

'I'm sure you're right, Godwin, it wasn't premeditated, at least not for long. This murder was a reaction to something that happened very recently. The key to it all is Nora.'

'I don't know. Nothing like this has happened in Ockendon in my time. I know you had a couple of murders over in Tennysham last spring and there's Brighton but not here. I was expecting a peaceful end to the year. No more'n moving on a drunk outside the Pheasant.'

'We all were, Constable. Talking of the pub, we called in at dinner-time. Tell me, who's the bandy-legged individual with a disreputable tweed hat? Ratty sort of face, sharp eyes and looked in need of a good wash… if that narrows it down?'

'Sounds like old Fly Carter,' Pickard said promptly.

'He didn't seem keen on meeting us. Slid out as soon as we came in.'

'Ah, that sounds about right. He's not called Fly on account of the ones in his hat. He's by far our worst local poacher, sir, and everyone knows who you are.'

Chance yawned. 'Where might I find him?'

'He'll be pottering about his place, this time of day. What would you want with him, sir?'

'Oh, a quick word. I thought he looked the type who might be out and about at night.'

'Not this week, Inspector. Poachers don't like full moon and the ground's frozen. Can't set snares if it's snowing.'

'I sit corrected. Where does he live?'

'Take the lane on the corner past the Pheasant and it's quarter-mile along. Last cottage on the right. You can't miss it, it's an eye-sore. Wouldn't be allowed on the green.'

'We'll toddle along there. I'm hoping my sergeant will be on the blower again. If he calls before we return, take down his message and thank him for me, will you?'

'I'll do that, sir. You're coming straight back here, are you, then?'

Godwin gave him a sympathetic grin.

~

They stood outside the shop while Chance opened his ten Players and looked at the card. The bell jangled on the door of the post-office and he raised his hat to a lady ushering her child over the step.

'We appear to be the star attraction.' He made a face at the little girl who'd turned round to stare at them. Mittens dangling from her sleeves on elastic, she grinned back at them.

They turned at the corner into a lane where the cottages were starting to straggle. Bare, thorny hedgerows looked like tangled barbed wire daubed with snow.

'It sounds as though the vicar's wife was very helpful,' Godwin said.

'If you want to know what's going on, consult an older woman. Someone kindly, if possible. An old cat will twist what they tell you and while men gossip as much as women, they notice a darned sight more than we do.'

'I've been thinking, sir.'

'Go on.'

'Could this be about the diamonds? What if the family are right and there was a jewel robbery that went wrong?'

'Nora on the inside and a falling out of thieves?'

'Yes, suppose she was meant to bring the Atherton diamonds outside but couldn't get them? She met her accomplice and he lost his temper?'

'It's a reasonable theory.'

Chance stopped at a barred gate, facing a view of flat, snowy fields. The Downs were behind them. Across to their left, he could see the yard behind the pub. Light spilled from an upstairs window over the slate roof of a lean-to. An arc of starlings crossed the pale sky and he could smell wood-smoke.

'Sir?'

He realised that Godwin had said something else. 'Eh?'

'Could that be right?'

'I can think of several possible motives, considering they're a small group of suspects.'

He saw the frustration on Godwin's face. 'Try going through them in turn.'

'Right, Gerald Clements has had a go at forging Clifford Vernon's signature. We don't know if he's actually used it but Nora had the evidence. Even though Mr. Vernon would be unlikely to prosecute, Clements would be disgraced. He'd lose his job, his comfortable home and possibly an inheritance.'

'Agreed. Next one?'

'Mrs Atherton has had an affair with Basil Mayhew. She doesn't want her husband to know. He might be a jealous type, despite her denial and it could be very embarrassing if Mrs Terry and Freda find out. It would probably ruin Mr. Atherton's friendship with the family and he might blame her. Did Nora know about their affair?'

'Quite likely, she may have overheard them talking or noticed something. Tate did and Nora obviously had an eye for opportunity.'

'Tate might have told his wife what he told you, sir and Nora listened in.'

Chance nodded encouragingly. 'Keep going.'

Godwin was counting off his gloved fingers. 'Looking at it the other way, Jimmy Atherton's just as likely. Suppose Nora told him about his wife and Mayhew, saying she'd keep quiet if he paid up? He could have had more than one reason for killing her. To save losing face? He feared his wife would run off with Mayhew if the affair was in the open? Or even to stop Freda Terry being hurt.'

'Any more for the dock?'

'Basil Mayhew, so he doesn't lose Freda Terry. She's likely to inherit from Clifford Vernon or her mother will. You think he's hard up, sir. I don't think he's in love with Freda.'

'Being a detective's made you cynical, Godwin. I agree Miss Terry deserves better.'

'Then we come to her. The only thing I can think of, is if Nora told her about Mayhew and Mrs Atherton. Either to ask for money to keep it quiet or just to be spiteful? If Freda Terry really loves Mayhew, she might have preferred to silence Nora.'

'From the way Miss Terry looks at Mayhew, I'd say she wants wedded bliss.' Chance stamped his feet. 'Getting parky, we'd better get on in a minute. What about the last two?'

'I can't come up with a motive for Mr. Vernon, or not one strong enough. Would he really go so far as murder to protect his niece or his old friend?'

'In a stage-play, he'd be the villain.' Chance watched his breath puff in the air.

'I can't come up with a motive for Beatrice Terry either.'

'Can't you?' Chance stepped back in the lane. 'Never underestimate the power of mother-love.'

The last cottage was made of wood with a mossy tin roof, its furrows ridged with snow. Smoke trickled from a metal chimney. House and fence had a knocked-together, make-do look. Rows of bedraggled Brussels sprouts sagged out of the snow. Chicken-wire separated the back garden and a henhouse. They could hear the sound of an axe working. A single bark sounded as they came through the gate. No dog appeared.

When they rounded the back of the cottage, the short figure from the pub was standing there, his axe resting on a neat stump sawn from a telegraph pole. A black and white mongrel, with a good dash of collie, watched them avidly.

'Ar'ternoon.'

The man, who could have been any age but young, touched a grubby finger to his cap. Wiry, with his skin the colour of tea, he waited, eyes as intelligent as his companion.

'Afternoon, Mr. Carter.' Chance raised his hat in return. 'You know who we are, I think?'

He nodded, keeping still. Not wary, Chance thought, simply waiting until he could return to his task. A pile of split logs were already stacked inside a porch.

'There's nothing I could tell you.'

'Did you know Nora Bennet to speak to?'

A dismissive shake of his head. 'Not since she were a nipper. I knew her father. They'll put her in with him and her ma, I suppose?'

'I expect so.'

Turning his head to one side, Carter spat into the snow. 'Be sure and get him.'

'Him?'

'Can't see a woman done it.' As if at some hidden signal, the dog moved over to him, standing against his legs. 'All right, girl?' He rubbed her head.

'I wondered if you might have been out at night lately?'

'Might have been. No law against being out after dark, even if Bert Pickard thinks there is.'

'Absolutely. A man's entitled to get some air when he likes.'

'Not what he reckons.'

'Frankly, Mr. Carter, I don't care if you've every pheasant in the district swinging in your larder. I hate doing paperwork, don't I, Constable?'

Godwin grinned. 'You're known for it, sir.'

'Were you out two nights ago, on the night of Boxing Day?'

'I was, as it happens, go out most nights.'

'Near Holly House at all?'

Carter nodded. 'Told you, I didn't see nothing. Far side of the river, I was, on the path through the spinney. And I weren't up to nothing, neither. Nothing you'd want to eat out and about when the ground's frozen. We saw the old dog fox, didn't we, Peg?'

At the sound of her name, his dog shoved her muzzle under his hand.

'Why were you out, then?' Chance said, interested.

The other man looked thoughtful. 'Habit,' he said, after a pause. 'I s'pose Peg and me have got our regular run, same as an old badger. I don't sleep much and I like being out in the small hours. There's a bit of peace to think in. T'aint the same indoors.'

'Know what time you were by the river?' Chance sounded careless.

'The church clock struck one when I turned away across the fields.'

'Did you see anyone on the other side, in the grounds of Holly House?'

A shake of the head. 'Didn't see no one.'

'Would your dog growl if anyone was about?'

'Only if a keeper were coming up behind me, like. She knows to stay quiet.'

'Did you see a light over there?'

'No need, three days off full moon.'

Chance grunted. 'It was worth asking. Thanks anyway.'

He and Godwin were turning away when the old poacher spoke again.

'Was someone else about.'

'What? Why didn't you say?'

Carter shifted his dog gently with the toe of his boot. 'Did I see 'un, you said. Somebody was coming along opposite, on the path that leads to the priory. And it weren't the old monk out walking. They were doing their best to keep quiet but we knew they were there.'

Godwin stepped forward. 'Have you any idea if they were a man or woman, Mr. Carter?'

'Told you, boy, Peg and me were going through the spinney. Sounds carry a long way at night, so do smells but I couldn't see 'un. They weren't having a smoke, I'll tell you that much.'

He began to gather the logs he'd chopped.

'Thanks for telling us,' Chance said simply.

'I'd hand 'em to you if I knew who. They deserve their neck wrung.' Carter grinned at them, revealing worn brown teeth. 'A man's feet, I reckon. But then again, you do get some heavy women.'

Chance looked back when they reached the gate where they'd stood. In a short time the sky had suffused with a first glow of rose-pink. Birds looked black in the distance.

'Nice place, he has. Don't turn your nose up, I bet he has everything just how he wants it. No one to make him clear up. That's a contented man, if I'm not mistaken.'

'I thought you'd get shirty because he didn't report hearing someone, sir?'

'We can't expect witnesses to find us and give us everything on a plate. It's our job to sniff them out. With a chap like that, there's absolutely no point in tearing them off a strip. He thinks of the village bobby, the way a hen thinks of the fox.'

'Do you think the murderer was a man, sir?'

'Anyone can use a catapult,' Chance said seriously. 'But a good eye helps.'

~

No more snow had fallen all day. Chance stood at the window of his room and thought about their progress. He went over his brief chat with his friend and sergeant, punctuated by the pushing of coins in a telephone box. The London streets, Bishop had said, were slippery with filthy slush. It was spitting with rain and the buses were packed in the West End.

He'd found out what was asked

Chance thought about his daughter, who didn't have to go into service. Godwin being glad to get back to his family, the Terrys and Gerald Clements being invited by Clifford Vernon to live at Holly House. Nora Bennet didn't sound an appealing young woman but she wasn't much more than a kid scrabbling for a home.

Below him, soft light reflected from the entrance and two men came out. They paused for a last word by the mounting block, then their footsteps went snapping down the street. A stumble and a muffled curse drifted back to him.

He was sure he knew.

Last Morning

The three of them left the police-house. Hands in pockets, Chance watched as P.C. Pickard stowed his spade and rake in the boot.

'Sure you know what you're looking for?'

'Greyish, smooth and round, 'bout the size of a gobstopper.'

'The snow was badly trampled when they removed the body but it'll be there somewhere.'

Godwin wiped the windscreen. The village seemed unnaturally still, no more snow overnight, nor any sign of thaw. No sign of life around the green and no birdsong.

He broke the quiet himself with the hollow throbbing of the engine. Chance sat next to him. Bert Pickard's white face in the mirror said he'd rather be somewhere else.

They drove through the deep shadow beneath the gatehouse, out into the harsh bluish white light of the morning. Chance had directed them to wait until breakfast at Holly House would be over. The Morgan was parked on the drive and Mayhew had one side of his bonnet up. He looked up as he heard them and folded it down, his face cheerful. He came up to them as they slowed past him and drew up. Pickard set about unloading his tools.

'Morning, back again, Inspector, with reinforcements? No offence but we thought we'd seen the back of you. What more can we tell you?'

'Mr. Mayhew.' Chance acknowledged him with a slight nod. 'You might be surprised how much people forget to say the first time.'

'That's not a dig at me, is it?'

'One of our London colleagues did have a word with your char-lady yesterday.'

Godwin watched Mayhew's face stiffen, almost comically. 'That's a damned cheek. You've no right to go snooping at my flat. You could get me thrown out.'

'Not to worry. As far as the lady's concerned, someone came round from the rates office with a survey. I wouldn't go sacking her, sir. It wouldn't look good if you've nothing to hide.'

'Look here, Inspector, your only interest is in catching the murderer. Anything else you find out is irrelevant. Surely you have a duty to keep it confidential?'

Chance took his time answering. 'As you say, we're only interested in who killed Nora Bennet. Going somewhere, Mr. Mayhew?'

'I was thinking of seeing how the roads are later. Only she tends to get a mite temperamental if she doesn't get started up for a few days. You interested in these, Constable?'

Godwin looked up from studying the dashboard. 'That's a beauty you've got there, Mr. Mayhew. An Aero, isn't she?'

Mayhew relaxed. 'She certainly is, four years old. They've just brought out a new model but this'll do me. If you appreciate motor-cars, it's a shame you can't see Jimmy

Atherton's great beast. He drives a Bentley Tourer but it's in dock. These machines are like women, the better-looking they are, the more unreliable. Anyway, I thought I'd see if Miss Terry fancies coming for a spin in a bit. That's if you've no objection, Inspector?'

'I'm afraid I must request you to stay within the grounds until we leave.'

'I say, what does that mean?'

Chance turned away dismissively. 'If you've quite finished drooling, Godwin, we've work to do.'

The butler must have been watching, for he opened the door as they approached.

'Will you let Mr. Vernon know we're here?' Chance said.

'Certainly, sir.'

'Tell him P.C Pickard is in the grounds. He'll be searching where the body was lying.'

The butler's eyes widened. 'Very good, Inspector Chance. I'll tell Mr. Vernon.'

'And is Mr. Clements about?'

'I believe he's in Mr. Vernon's study. This way, if you please.'

Godwin tucked his brief-case beneath his arm as he followed. The corridor was lined with old sporting prints, delicately tinted. He glanced at boxing, cricket, steeplechasing and fishing, before they reached a door where Tate knocked and showed them in.

Gerald Clements dropped his pen on his blotter and half-rose as they entered.

An expensive pen, Godwin thought, as he fetched himself a chair from against the wall. The room was spacious and comfortable, no sign of a typewriter. The wall behind the desk was all bookshelves. An oil-painting of the priory, the walls somewhat higher, hung opposite the window.

'What is it this time?' Clements sounded resigned.

'Writing a letter, sir?'

'Nothing important. None of us know what to do with ourselves. It doesn't seem quite the thing to go out or play music and the guests are unable to leave.'

'Mr. Mayhew's the only one likely to be called at the inquest.'

'Even so. I should think the Athertons could get up to town now but Jimmy won't desert my uncle and Bea. They've taken this very hard.'

At his signal, Godwin opened his brief-case and passed Chance the sheet of paper. He placed the sheet in front of Clements without speaking. The secretary's face drained of colour.

'Where did you get this?'

'Detective Constable Godwin found it hidden among Nora's effects.'

Clements swallowed. 'What happens now?'

'Now you tell us all about it.'

'I didn't know she had this, I swear. So I had no reason to kill Nora, I never laid a finger on her.'

Chance regarded him steadily. 'When did you miss this?'

'I... I didn't miss it. It was ages ago, this isn't what it seems. It's all perfectly innocent.'

'Come off it. You'll be telling us you were doodling next. I'm sure Mr. Vernon would like to see your artistic efforts. After all, you've taken a lot of trouble.'

'No... please, Inspector, hear me out.'

'I'm listening.'

Godwin wondered, not for the first time, if he had the stomach for the job.

'I needed some money. I knew my uncle wouldn't give me an advance on my salary, he'd cut up rough once before. He simply doesn't understand how expensive things are. He's quite happy mouldering away down here. So I um...' Clements ran his tongue round his lips. 'You know what I thought.'

'You'd pay yourself an advance. Save your uncle writing the cheque?'

He nodded. 'I didn't go through with it, I assure you. A friend repaid a loan and I forgot all about it.' He waved a hand at the blotter. 'This was in my room in my private desk. I didn't think I needed to lock it. The little bitch was always hanging around. She must have gone through my papers.'

'How long ago?'

Clements shrugged, 'October.'

'Are you willing to make a statement to the effect that Nora Bennet did not attempt to blackmail you?'

'Yes, if you keep this quiet, I'll sign anything.'

'So it seems,' Chance said. 'Come on, Godwin, we've wasted enough time.'

~

Elsie Ruddock was wiping a breakfast plate when she heard Mrs Tate speak to someone. She'd just spotted a smear of egg yolk dried on the rim and was chipping it off with her fingernail. A deep, man's voice sent her nipping to the scullery door, tea cloth in hand.

The plain-clothes policeman was standing there, still in his overcoat, with the young chap hovering at his side.

'And this must be Mrs Ruddock.'

'That's me.'

A Sussex accent but quite nicely-spoken with it. He was a cut above Bert Pickard.

'Splendid, I'm hoping one of you can help me.'

'We'll do our best, sir.' Mrs Tate stood by the table.

'This may seem strange but bear with me. We have to ask all sorts of peculiar questions.'

Elsie stepped closer, the dishes could wait.

'If you think back to the morning Nora's body was discovered, do either of you recall in what order the household got up?'

Mrs Tate frowned. 'My husband is always up first as a rule, though Mr. Vernon's an early riser. Tate brings me a cup of tea and we're out here by half-past six. Our flat's on the ground floor.'

'I was here by eight. I'm up here every day while they've guests.'

The inspector smiled at her. He had his own teeth. 'You must be particularly busy and I've taken you away from your work.'

'That's all right, sir. It was a dreadful shock when Nora was murdered. I'm sure I haven't felt the same since. I come all over cold when Miss Freda ran in to tell us.'

He looked concerned. 'Shock's a very nasty thing, Mrs Ruddock.'

Mrs Tate made a tetchy sound in her throat. 'We mustn't keep the gentleman waiting, Elsie. Now, sir, I think I can tell you what you asked. Mrs Terry and Mr. Vernon came down together with Miss Freda soon after. Then came Mr. Mayhew and Mr. Atherton. He was down before his wife. Mr. Clements came later, he has a job to wake up these dark mornings.'

'Mrs Atherton was last by a long chalk. I couldn't get the table cleared and then when she did come down, all she wanted was coffee. Said she felt groggy and couldn't face anything solid. Must have been those cocktails.'

Mrs Tate shot her an old-fashioned look but she wouldn't be kept from speaking up. It was their duty to help the police.

'You've both been very helpful. Made a note of all that, Constable?'

'Sir.'

That young chap still looked wet behind the ears. His boss gave her a lovely smile. He had the measure of Hilda Tate.

~

'So far, so good,' Chance said. 'Let's find Vernon.'

Clifford Vernon and Beatrice Terry were speaking to Tate in the library. They broke off as soon as they saw the detectives.

'Ah, Inspector Chance. I understand P.C. Pickard is searching by the ruins? May we ask what this means?'

'We're looking for part of the murder weapon.'

'A part, you say?'

'That's right, sir. The murderer replaced the weapon itself over there.' Chance gestured down the room. 'Nora Bennet was killed with your catapult.'

There was a suppressed movement from Tate. Mrs Terry gripped her brother's sleeve.

Vernon stared at Chance. 'It must be fifty years old. It was in one of the out-houses when I came here, along with the fisherman's priest. I kept them as curios. Late Victorian rural tools as described by Jefferies. Good grief, catapults, or slingshots, were designed to bring down birds.'

'Still in use,' Chance said. 'Perfectly made to despatch swiftly and silently. I met your village poacher yesterday, I'm sure he'll have his own. Perhaps you'd come and look at your musket balls for me. I'd like you to count them.'

Vernon patted his sister's hand and removed it gently. He drew back his stooped shoulders and looked Chance in the eye. 'Certainly. There should be fourteen.'

'Do you mind if I sit down?'

Beatrice Terry sank on to the edge of the sofa, her face ashen.

'Tate, fetch a glass of water for Mrs Terry.' Vernon's voice was quietly authoritative.

'At once, sir.' Tate bowed and left.

'Will you be all right, ma'am?' Godwin lingered by the sofa as Vernon and Chance went over to the display-case.

'Yes, thank you, Constable. It's hearing the actual details. You go on.'

Chance raised his eyebrows at him as he joined them in the window. After what seemed a lengthy pause, Vernon straightened up.

'It seems you're quite correct, Inspector. Three are missing. All are the larger examples.'

'Thank you, sir. I understand this is difficult for you both.'

'Not your fault, Inspector.' He led them back towards his sister. 'Can you tell us what happens now?'

'I'd like your permission for us to search the bedroom wardrobes.' Chance looked over at Tate as he entered. 'That doesn't include the staff.'

'If it's necessary, then yes. Do what you must.'

'Excuse me, Mr. Vernon.'

'Yes, Tate, what is it?'

'I believe Mrs Atherton is in her bedroom. Would you like me to appraise her of the situation and suggest she'd be more comfortable downstairs?'

'Yes, do that now. Should we keep this to ourselves, Inspector?'

'I'd rather you inform the household of developments, if you will. And if anyone is thinking of going for a walk, perhaps you'd instruct them to stay here. I've spoken to Mr. Mayhew. We'll do our best to cause a minimum of disturbance. Thank you for your cooperation, sir.'

'Shall I see you up there, sir?'

Chance nodded to him. 'I'll join you shortly.'

Vernon removed his spectacles and produced his handkerchief. 'Frankly, I'm at a loss to know what we should do. Shall you want us all to gather together, Inspector?'

'That won't be necessary, sir. They only do that in detective stories.' Chance looked at Mrs Terry, holding her glass. 'Might I have a brief word, ma'am?'

~

When they went outside, some half-hour later, a watery sunlight had broken through the clouds. The sparrows were back, squabbling among the bushes. The icicles beneath the eaves were dripping. They paused by the Morgan.

'I'll be glad when today's over, sir.'

'Not long now. We'll be back home enjoying our supper tonight.' Chance glanced at the house behind them. 'These poor devils won't have much appetite.'

Godwin hesitated. 'Do you ever think about it, sir? That we're responsible for sending someone to the rope?'

'The courts do that, not us. And if people will murder...' Chance shrugged. 'I never think about it,' he lied. 'Take my tip, Godwin, don't go all philosophical.' He was longing to smoke. 'It doesn't help.'

The snow was crossed by footprints again, at least three people. Word had got round. Chance picked out the marks where P.C. Pickard had used his spade as a walking-stick and let the rake trail behind him.

At the yew arch, they could see Pickard among snow raked into grubby ridges and an area of starched-looking grass. Jimmy Atherton and Freda Terry were talking to him. They looked round and Pickard straightened up, rubbing his back.

'No luck yet, sir,' he said as they approached.

'No matter,' Chance said. 'Godwin found one.'

'P.C. Pickard won't tell us what he's looking for,' Freda Terry said.

'This.' Chance opened his palm and showed her a spherical musket ball. About the size of a large gob-stopper, it was the colour of putty.

'What on earth..?'

Freda broke off as Atherton rushed forward and grabbed the rake, brandishing the tined end at them.

'Jimmy, what are you doing?'

Ignoring her, Atherton backed away, holding them at bay, though no one else moved. His eyes flickered like a startled horse and he glanced behind him towards the drive. 'Keep away, I warn you!'

'It's no good, Mr. Atherton.' Chance held up Basil Mayhew's key fob. 'It's all over. You forgot the spare musket balls when you replaced the catapult. We've just found one in the pocket of your trousers. The pair with a trace of staining on them. The lab will prove they're lichen from the wall. Best put that down.'

Freda stared at the men. 'You can't possibly think... Jimmy, tell them for God's sake.'

'I didn't want to kill her. I had no choice.' Atherton's chest was heaving.'

Chance knew he was still thinking of running. He looked around rapidly. A movement among the ruins caught his eye. Couldn't get near enough to tackle Atherton, he put out his arm to keep Godwin back.

'Freda, please, don't look at me like that. Go back and keep Lois away. She can't see me like this. Go, I'm begging you. Look after her.'

Freda stared at him, white-faced, spun round to the others. 'What do I do?'

'Go inside,' Chance said quietly.

She hurried across to the opening in the hedge, almost stumbling, not glancing back.

'Now come on, be sensible,' Pickard said. 'Just you put that down and come with us. You don't want to make a show. It won't do you any good.'

'Get back, I say.' Atherton jabbed the rack at Pickard as he stepped forward. 'I need to make you see. I'm not a murderer, I'm really not.'

They edged nearer each time Atherton backed away. Chance thought of how they'd seem to onlookers, like some bizarre game of *Grandmother's footsteps*.

'You must have planned to kill Nora,' he said.

Atherton was near the wall he'd climbed along that night.

'I had to keep her quiet. I had to stop Lois from finding out. I did plan it but only over a day. If I'd thought the girl could be trusted to say nothing, I'd have bought her off somehow but she kept sneering. I knew there was only one way.'

'Why did you do it?' Pickard threw the C.I.D. men a surly look.

Chance knew he didn't appreciate not being taken into their confidence. Too bad. Every sinew in his body felt ready to move.

Atherton shook his head violently, his face anguished. 'It doesn't matter now.'

'You've lost all your money,' Chance said.

'How did you find out?'

'Your car for one thing.'

In one fluid movement, Atherton hurled the rake at the constable and ran the last few yards. Pickard floundered in the snow in front of them, hampering them as they dodged round him. By the time Godwin and Chance reached the foot of the priory wall, Atherton was scrambling frantically. He kicked out at Godwin's upstretched wrist, sending him over, and was out of reach. Pickard got to his feet, brushing and cursing.

Chance stared up, his lungs feeling painful from such a brief exertion. The other two joined him, Godwin holding his wrist. Pickard cricked his neck and bellowed.

'You come down from there, d'you hear me? There's nowhere you can go.'

Atherton peered down at them from almost the highest part of the ruin. He'd reached one of the few remaining ledges of an upper window along the nave.

Safe for the moment, clutching an upright stone support which had once held glass. Pickard was right, Chance thought. Atherton could climb like a cat but he'd run out of footholds. He'd have to be talked down.

'I saw the log-book in the Austin. The constable here said you drive a Bentley. Even I know they're a rich man's choice. So I wondered why you hired a small motor-car to drive down from London.'

'I told my wife something was up with the Bentley.' Atherton's eyes were fixed on him.

'My sergeant's up in the Smoke. He spoke to the chap where you garage the Bentley. For the past month, it's been up for sale in the window of a West End show-room near your home.'

Atherton groaned.

'On the morning of the twenty-seventh, when Nora's body was found, your wife was last down to breakfast. Even though she tended to rise late, she complained of feeling groggy. Mr. Vernon said she had a bad headache all day. I think you gave her one of your sleeping-powders in a bedtime drink, so she wouldn't wake up on Boxing night and find you were gone.'

'I couldn't risk her waking and wondering where I was. I'd never hurt her.'

'But she did wonder, Mr. Atherton. She went into Nora's room yesterday morning to see if she could find anything that incriminated you. She didn't know what she was looking for but she's no fool. I think she suspected you drugged her and murdered Nora.'

Atherton's eyes closed for an instant. 'Lois can't think that of me, she can't.'

'How long have you had trouble sleeping?' Chance said.

'It's been months now, before I met my wife. I've been dogged with money worries. I've lost everything but I thought I could recover, if I could only hold on. I couldn't bear anyone knowing I've been such a fool. I didn't even notice it slipping away at first, then my broker warned me. It's been happening ever since the Crash. Land isn't worth a fraction of what it was before the War. My investments are virtually worthless. I've lost a bundle on plays that dived, shares have been wiped out. Then I met Lois and it seemed like a miracle. She made me so happy.'

'Why not tell her the truth?'

'Because I couldn't bear to lose her. I've no illusions, she could have any man her own age and she chose me. I believe she's genuinely fond of me and that's enough. But Lois wouldn't look twice at me if I was poor. How could I let her know my life had become a sham? She's had a rotten time and money makes her feel safe.'

'Why not bring yourself down and you can talk to her? Put things square between you.'

He shook his head vehemently. 'I don't want her to see me like this. It's too late.'

'I know Nora found out your secret. You lied about catching her trying on your wife's coat on Christmas afternoon. You told me you saw Nora through the half-open bedroom door and she was admiring herself in the wardrobe mirror. The wardrobe's in the far corner. You couldn't possibly have seen her from the door. You had to tell us something because Mrs Terry was coming up the stairs and you weren't sure if she heard you and Nora arguing.'

'You seem to have it all worked out.'

'Not everything. Mrs Terry recalled Nora leaving your room but she didn't hear you by the way, I asked her earlier.'

'Oh God. I did think there was a risk she'd heard us.'

'Will you tell us how Nora found out? We know she snooped among guests' things. Did she read a letter?'

'No, I had nothing like that with me. I caught her with my wife's diamonds. It was such a stupid thing. She was scratching one of the stones on the window-pane when I walked in. She had hold of that old tale about only a diamond being hard enough to scratch glass. She guessed they're paste.'

Chance felt Pickard shift in surprise beside him. His neck ached, his attention was fixed on Atherton above him and the ruins.

Atherton went on. 'I had to have a copy made, the necklace is a family piece. I was forced to sell the real diamonds last year. Then I had to give Lois a decent wedding present and a gift for Christmas. They're paste too. I told myself I'd replace them when things picked up. She'd never know.'

'Surely you tried to tell Nora she was mistaken?'

'Of course I tried but she wouldn't believe me. You don't know what she was like, Chance. You didn't meet her. She went on and on at me, grinning and taunting. She was longing to tell Lois. If I'd been quicker, I'd have told her Lois knew but I couldn't think quickly enough. Everything's been going round and round in my head for months, like a rat in a trap.'

'None of that's any excuse for murder,' Pickard had his hands on his hips. 'You're only making things worse for yourself. We can stand here all night if we have to.'

'Shut up,' Chance said.

Pickard subsided, his mouth tight.

'Tell us the rest, Mr. Atherton. I think you want to.'

'I do want you to know, Chance. I'm not an evil man. I manged to get her quiet by saying I'd pay her. I convinced her I could get hold of some money, once we were back in town. She agreed but said she wanted something before then. I said I'd get a loan from Cliff, he keeps some in his safe but I needed to find the best time to ask. It was Christmas Day for God's sake. She agreed to give me a day and it was her suggestion we meet here after everyone had gone to bed on Boxing night. She said it was too risky to talk in the house. It was all a game to her.'

'So you edged along this wall, rather lower than you are now, with the catapult?'

Atherton nodded miserably. 'It sounds insane now but I had a night and a day to think it up. I thought if she could be found dead without any other tracks, everyone would assume she'd hit her head. I remembered the catapult and I was always a keen bowler. Hitting a target's no problem to me. She died instantly. I didn't want her to suffer, just leave me alone for ever. I'm so very tired.'

There was a flurry of movement and Mrs Atherton stepped out from behind an arch. She halted between the wall and Chance, looking up at her husband.

Chance thought her face ghastly beneath the rouge. He could see the woman she'd be in another ten years.

'Lois, my darling, I don't want you to see me like this.' Atherton clung to the stonework. 'I'm so sorry, my love. I've let you down. How long have you been there?'

'Long enough.' She shoved her hands in her coat pockets to stop them shaking.

'It was all for you, my darling. I wanted to keep you safe.'

She looked up at him. 'You murdered some poor, stupid, little kid on the make. I was probably no better than Nora when I was young.'

'Don't say that. She was nothing like you. She left me with no choice.'

Mrs Atherton's voice shook. 'There's always a choice. You bloody fool, Jimmy. I'd have scrubbed floors for you. It was all for nothing.'

She turned her back on him, gave Chance and the others a scornful look and walked away.

~

'I thought he was going to jump,' Godwin said.

They were standing in the entrance to the police-station yard. Chance's cigarette smoke drifted towards the empty buildings opposite.

'So did I, just before he started weeping. I thought Atherton would make right for the top when his wife left and you'd have to swarm up there like a monkey.'

'Me, sir?'

'Privileges of rank. Besides, I don't like heights.'

Back in Tennysham, the tide was out. The snow had turned to greyish slush on the pavements, with the roads filthy. A crowd was queuing outside the new picture-house, as they'd driven past. At the theatre, they were hooking back the doors for the panto and outside the town-hall, the posters were up for the mayor's New Year ball.

Funny how different things could seem after two nights away.

'What d'you think will become of Mrs Atherton, sir?'

'Same as any of us,' Chance said. 'We simply keep trying.'

He tossed his cigarette-end and watched a shower of tiny glowing sparks extinguish on the grubby street.

The End

By the same author

The Seafront Corpse

Set in 1931, newly promoted Inspector Eddie Chance is back in his home town. Reunited with his old pal Sergeant Bishop in the sleepy Sussex town of Tennysham-on-Sea. The only cloud on their horizon is a young police-woman with ambitions to be a detective. The seaside resort is getting ready for the first day trippers of the season. When the body of a stranger is found on the promenade, Inspector Chance is faced with a baffling murder... A traditional 1930s murder mystery set in a vanished England of typewriters, telephone boxes and tweeds.

A Seaside Mourning

An intriguing Victorian murder mystery. Autumn 1873. Inspector Josiah Abbs and Sergeant Ned Reeve are sent to investigate their first case of murder. At the small town of Seaborough, on the Devon coast, a wealthy spinster has died suddenly in suspicious circumstances. Some locals have ambitious plans to see the seaside resort expand. Was Miss Chorley killed because she stood in their way? Or beneath the elaborate rituals of mourning, does the answer lie closer to home? Behind the Nottingham lace curtains, residents and visitors have their schemes and secrets. The two detectives must untangle the past to find answers. When a second body is found, time is running out to solve a baffling mystery. But uncovering the truth may prove dangerous...

A Christmas Malice

December 1873. Inspector Abbs is visiting his sister in a lonely village on the edge of the Norfolk Fens. He is hoping for a quiet week while he thinks over a decision about his future. However all is not well in Aylmer. Someone has been playing malicious tricks on the inhabitants. With time on his hands and concerned for his sister, Abbs feels compelled to investigate.

Speak for the Dead

Secrets and murder in the fog of Victorian London. When a grieving architect is stabbed by an intruder, the case seems simple enough. Only Inspector Josiah Abbs begs to differ. A stranger at Scotland Yard, Abbs must untangle a web of secrets and deceit, to find a murderer and make his mark. In 1874, the Metropolis is changing, as streets are torn down and new buildings put up by the month. Meanwhile, in public halls and darkened parlours, the spiritualist movement is at its height… Finding his way about the fog-shrouded city, Abbs will risk everything to get justice for the dead.

You can contact Anne Bainbridge at:
gaslightcrime@yahoo.co.uk

Printed in Great Britain
by Amazon